"Safety in numbers?"

Vere quirked an eyebrow as he voiced the mocking query.

"I'm a big girl now." Fabienne laughed.

"I—" Vere began. And then his look decidedly cool, "Are you saying you have frequent affairs?"

Her jaw dropped. Never had she known anyone so forthright. "No, I'm not!" she retorted—not that it was any of his business if she did!

"Might I remind you that I'm your employer?" he rapped.

"So fire me!" she erupted.

Jessica Steele lives in a friendly Worcestershire village with her super husband, Peter. They are owned by a gorgeous Staffordshire bull-terrier called Daisy, who thinks she's human—they don't like to tell her otherwise.

It was Peter who first prompted Jessica to try writing, and after the first rejection, encouraged her to keep on trying. With Uruguay the exception, she has so far managed to research inside all the countries in which she has set her books. Her thanks go to Peter for his help and encouragement.

Books by Jessica Steele

BACHELOR'S FAMILY
Jessica Steele

Harlequin Books

TORONTO • NEW YORK • LONDON
AMSTERDAM • PARIS • SYDNEY • HAMBURG
STOCKHOLM • ATHENS • TOKYO • MILAN
MADRID • WARSAW • BUDAPEST • AUCKLAND

ISBN 0-373-03356-7

BACHELOR'S FAMILY

Copyright © 1995 by Jessica Steele.

First North American Publication 1995.

CHAPTER ONE

FABIENNE had said cheerio to her parents and Oliver, their mischievous Jack Russell terrier, and was in the hall on her way to spend Saturday evening with some of her friends when the phone rang. 'I'll get it!' she called, and went over to the instrument, picked it up, and said, 'Hello.'

'Miss Preston?' queried an all-masculine, all-authoritative voice. A voice she immediately recognised, for all she had only heard it once before.

'Y-yes,' she stammered, and could barely believe that, when she was normally so confident, she should sound so nervous!

'Vere Tolladine.' He announced that which she already knew.

'Oh, yes,' she replied guardedly.

'Can you start Monday?'

'I've got the job?'

'Don't you want it?' There it was again, that brusque, no-nonsense tone she had brought on herself at the job interview.

'Of course I do!' she asserted, rattled, when in truth she had been unsure. But, not one to be oppressed by anyone, she metaphorically pulled up her socks and, before he could bark out his orders on what time she should start on Monday, she took the battle straight into his camp. 'If I'm to get the twins to school for nine, I'd better move in tomorrow,' she declared.

'Do that,' he returned coolly, and spent the next few minutes giving her directions on how to get to

Brackendale, his home in the village of Sutton Ash, Berkshire, from her home in the small town of Lintham, Oxfordshire. 'Until Sunday,' he ended—and put down his phone.

Slowly, Fabienne did the same. But, even as she pondered why she should have considered her dealings with Vere Tolladine as a battle, she knew that she was committed. Too late now to consider if she really and positively wanted the job of 'temporary nanny and mother's help' she had seen advertised. In all honesty, though, she hadn't thought, when she'd journeyed to London for an 'expenses-paid' interview, that she had stood a chance of getting it. For she had not the smallest nanny-mother's help credential. Her only experience of the workplace was as first assistant in her mother's gown shop.

'Who was it?' Her mother and Oliver, coming out into the hall from the drawing-room, caused Fabienne to concentrate her thoughts on how in creation she was to soften the blow that, albeit temporarily, she was leaving home.

There was, she swiftly realised as she bent to pat Oliver absently, no way to soften it. 'You know that interview I went for last Tuesday? Well,' she went on quickly, not wanting to draw out the agony, 'I got the job.'

'Oh, love!' Clare Preston cried, but proved again what Fabienne already knew—that her mother was a special kind of person—for she suddenly found a smile and asked, 'Have you time to come and chat it over with your father and me before you go out?'

When, fifteen minutes later, Fabienne drove off to keep her arrangement with her friends, she took with her her parents' blessing about her leaving home to take up her new job.

It had helped, of course, that the job was temporary. And the fact that she was able to tell them that she would have every weekend off to come home went a long way to weaken their resistance. And, although she was twenty-two and of an age where she did not need her parents' consent to leave home, what finally convinced her father that she would come to no harm living in a household which was not his was that Vere Tolladine was known to him. Not that the two had ever met, but apparently the man who headed Tolladine Finance Incorporated was well known for his integrity in the business world—word of that integrity filtering down to her father who, with her brother Alex, ran the family engineering firm that touched the fringes of 'big' business. It was her father's view that Vere Tolladine's business integrity was so much part and parcel of the man that it must spill over into his private and, therefore, home life.

Fabienne halted her car in the car park of the George Hotel where she was meeting her friends. She did not immediately get out, however, but sat and reflected about how, save for her good friend Hannah, everyone in their group had left home ages ago and was now living on their own.

'Your parents make life too comfortable for you,' Tom Walton—another of her very good friends—had teased one time and, she realised, she could not argue with that.

She came from a very comfortable home and, from day one, had been loved, cared for and protected. Even her brother Alex, her senior by ten years, had taken to watching over her and was ever-ready to take up cudgels on her behalf.

It was Alex to whom she had turned when her studies at school were almost completed. She knew that her father was keen for her to go to the same university as

Alex and obtain an engineering degree with a view to entering the family firm. And Alex was, too. But, while she had no idea what sort of career she wanted, or if she wanted a career at all, what she did know was that she did not want to be an engineer. The problem was that as she was loved by her family, so she loved them as much in return, and she just could not bear the thought of hurting her father by telling him of her feelings.

Alex was married by that time and, after weeks of fretting about how to tell her father, it had all come blurting out one early evening when her brother came to collect her to babysit while he and his wife, Victoria, went for a rare evening out.

'Would Daddy be very upset if I didn't come into the firm, do you think?' she had said in a rush, before Alex had barely driven out of the avenue where she lived.

By the time they had reached the crescent where Alex lived, he had taken a tremendous load of worry from her by assuring her that their father would be twice as hurt if she went into training for something she had no appetite for, just to please him.

'Don't worry about it any more, Fenne,' Alex had said and, like the marvellous big brother he was, 'I'll tell Dad tomorrow, if you like.'

And she had been so relieved she had almost let him. But she was growing up and she just knew that this was something she must do for herself. 'No, I'll do it,' she'd replied.

Though she afterwards wondered if perhaps Alex had laid some sort of foundation for her, because when the very next evening she took her courage in both hands and tentatively began to tell her father how she felt, instead of being shocked, hurt and disappointed as she'd imagined he would be, for some serious moments he had looked solemnly into her worried brown eyes. Then, stretching out an arm to give her a hug, 'Is this your way of telling me you want to work in your mother's frock shop?' he'd teased.

'She'd scalp you if she heard you call Clare's a frock shop!' Fabienne had laughed in her relief—and, when she left school, somehow found that she *was* working, quite happily, in the gown shop which her mother had opened ten years previously.

Everything had gone along swimmingly, and was still going along swimmingly until some months ago when something had happened which had caused Fabienne to do some very in-depth thinking. Although, in fact, what she had had to do did not require very much thinking about at all.

Out of the blue her mother suddenly began to have dizzy spells. It was when she fainted outright, however, that her husband put his foot down.

The end result was that a medical consultant was called in, who said that there was nothing wrong that tablets and complete and utter rest would not cure. His stipulation that she must slow down and rest more in future, too, gave them all food for thought.

'I'm not very happy about your mother starting work again,' Edward Preston took his daughter aside one day to state.

Fabienne wasn't happy about it either, yet they were a work-orientated family and, despite this being Nature's way of telling her mother to slow down, her mother was already making noises to the effect that she'd had enough rest. 'How do you think she'd feel about closing the shop?' she asked him.

'Close the shop!'

'Mum will never rest while it's still open.'

'That's true,' her father conceded. 'What about you, though? Don't *you* want to keep it on?'

'It wouldn't work.'

'I can set you up in something of your own, if you like,' he offered.

'Can you see Mum resting while I'm rushing around in the throes of getting everything ready to open?' Fabienne vetoed that idea and, because her mother was going to be upset at the idea of closing down Clare's while there was any chance of keeping it open, 'Actually, I wouldn't mind having a go at something a bit different.'

What that something different was, however, she had little idea. She knew that she did not want to work in an office environment, nor a factory environment, either. Their own shop was closed down by then, but to work in someone else's gown shop, when she was used to virtually being her own boss, was something she felt would not work out very well either.

'What you need,' her friend Hannah stated after some thought, 'is a job that's a total contrast.'

'So tell me about it?' Fabienne encouraged.

'Something—something you wouldn't think of doing in a million years.'

'I'm not going deep-sea fishing for you or anybody,' Fabienne laughed.

Though it was Hannah who, a day or so later, produced the 'temporary nanny' advertisement. 'Have you seen this?' she asked, and didn't seem to think the notion was at all as preposterous as Fabienne did as she read the advertisement for a live-in, weekends-off, temporary nanny-cum-help to mother and seven-year-old twins during the school summer holidays. Interviewing expenses paid.

'Go back to sleep, Hannah,' was her initial reaction. But she went home with the piece of paper bearing the advertisement which Hannah had insisted she not dismiss out of hand, but think about. It was certainly a job that was a total contrast, she'd give Hannah that!

She was amused by Hannah's idea that she could do a nanny's job, or that anyone might want to employ her as such, and at dinner told her parents of her friend's latest wacky notion.

'What does she use for a brain?' was her father's good-humoured reaction.

'Actually, Hannah's got quite a good brain,' Fabienne defended. 'It's just that...'

'In this instance she left it in neutral.'

'Oh, I don't know, Edward,' her mother chipped in. 'Fabienne's very good with children. Her patience with Philip was endless when his "terrible twos" seemed to go on until he was five. Victoria couldn't do...' Her voice petered out, and they each became engrossed in their own thoughts for the moment.

Her parents adored Philip, their grandson; they all did. But, after Alex and Victoria had divorced last year, they saw less and less of him. The break-up of her brother's marriage had been bitter and acrimonious and the divorce messy, with Alex losing the fight for custody of his son and with Victoria, regardless of his 'rights of access', being obstructive when he went to collect Philip on his allotted weekend.

It was sad because they were all fond of Victoria, and they'd had no idea that there was anything wrong. It hadn't been until Victoria had started to complain about her husband working too many hours and the lack of a social life that they'd realised his marriage was hitting troubled waters. Just the same, it had been something of a very great shock when her mother had hinted to

Alex that it was three weeks since they'd seen Philip and Alex had confessed that Victoria had left the marital home, taking Philip with her, a month before. They later discovered that there was another man involved but, prior to obtaining her divorce, Victoria had been very circumspect about him.

Unusually, Fabienne had difficulty in sleeping that night and, when counting sheep proved useless, she gave her mind over to other matters, and found she was reflecting on the easy and happy relationship she had with her nephew. From there her thoughts went to the advert Hannah had given her—and suddenly the idea of applying for it did not seem anywhere near as absurd as it had initially.

When Fabienne left her bed the next morning she discovered that, far from forgetting all about the notion, she had remembered it. Remembered and, since she felt she had been idle for quite long enough, felt inclined to do something about it. 'You know, Mum,' she addressed her parent, 'I think I'll apply for that temporary nanny's job.'

Her mother threw her a startled look while her father, on his way out to work, plainly of the view that she was becoming as nutty as her friend, opined, 'You're seeing too much of that Hannah Reed!' and, giving his wife a kiss, departed.

To everyone's astonishment, Fabienne included, she had a letter on Saturday calling her to interview at a smart hotel in London the following Wednesday. Oh, crumbs, Fabienne thought as she read her letter from one Sonia Morris, now what did she do?

On the basis that it was some small while since she'd been to London, and that she would quite enjoy a look around the shops, she decided she could fit in the interview without too much hindrance to her trip.

It was early June, and the Wednesday dawned brightly and, since she guessed it was going to be hot in London, Fabienne opted for a long, loose-fitting print dress and sandals. She wondered if she should pin her long black hair back—braid it or something—but decided she fancied wearing it loose.

'You're going for a job interview like that?' her mother exclaimed, just as she was about to leave her elegant home on the outskirts of Lintham. 'You look like a gypsy!'

'How many gypsies do you know?' Fabienne countered with a laugh, and drove off to Oxford where she parked her car and took a train to London.

She entered the hotel with five minutes to spare before the appointed time and told the man at Reception that she was there to see a Mrs Morris. He had been forewarned to expect her, it seemed, for, 'May I have your name?' he enquired.

'Fabienne Preston,' she replied, and stood by the desk while he busied himself with the telephone and, after replacing it, summoned a page to escort her.

The hotel was smart and discreetly expensive and as Fabienne sailed upwards in the lift, so she began to wish—as her mother's 'gypsy' remark came back to her—that she had put on any other of the plentiful supply of smart clothes she had in her wardrobe.

Particularly did she wish it when a woman a few years older than herself, smart and efficiently clad in crisp linen, came from a door further up the corridor. Fabienne instinctively knew that she had just come from interview. They passed and she was even more certain, when she saw the woman's mousy hair was strictly gathered into a severe knot at the back of her head, that the woman had applied for, and had probably got, the temporary nanny's job.

It did not surprise her at all when the page stopped outside the door that the woman had just come from. 'Thank you.' She smiled to him, knocked, and waited.

The door was soon opened and a last-word-in-smartness woman stood there. 'Miss Preston?' she smiled. 'Come in.'

She led the way into the ante-room of a hotel suite—and that was when Fabienne realised that whoever got the job would not be working for any harassed mother on a budget. Not that she had thought about it much before; she had just sort of assumed that the interview would take place in the hotel lounge, perhaps over a cup of coffee. But Mrs Morris had clearly rented a suite and, in this hotel, that wouldn't come cheap.

'I think I'd better tell you, Mrs Morris, that——'

'Miss Morris,' the other replied and, while Fabienne was taking that on board, Sonia Morris smiled and at once disabused her of any idea that she was either a single lady or used the 'Miss' title for career purposes, by adding, 'I don't think we should keep him waiting.'

Waiting! She was bang on time, not so much as half a minute late. What sort of impatient person was she to see? And—*him*!

'You can tell Mr Tolladine what you have to during your interview,' Sonia Morris added serenely as she went over and opened a door that led into a room that was the main sitting-room of the suite. 'Miss Fabienne Preston, Mr Tolladine,' she announced and, ushering her in, she promptly went from the room, closing the door after her.

In those initial moments of looking across at the dark-haired man, probably about thirty-five, who stood well above average height, and who looked back at her with the most direct look from cool grey eyes, Fabienne went through the whole gamut of thoughts and emotions.

Where was Mrs Tolladine? She'd have thought, since it was *her* she or the successful applicant would be working with, that the twins' mother would want to interview her in person. Though on looking at the cool, grey-eyed man, Fabienne had a notion that one would have to be up very early in the morning to put one over on him!

Whether he was used to interviewing nannies on his wife's behalf, she had no idea, but she quickly formed the notion that he was more than up to the job. There was a tough look about that strong, firm chin that said he did not suffer fools gladly and, as she saw the immaculately suited man take in her smooth, olive-tinted complexion, brown eyes, loose-flowing hair and dress to match—his one glance taking in her classic but none the less casual sandals and bare toes—so she began to feel at a disadvantage and, more than ever then, wished she had dressed differently.

'I shouldn't have come!' she stated, her voice strangely husky, as she half turned to the door.

'Why?' Just the one word. Curt. Crisp. No-nonsense. It stopped her.

'Because——' She turned to face him, and stayed to tell him what she had been on the way to telling Sonia Morris a few minutes ago. 'Because I don't have one single solitary qualification for the job.'

For a stern second or two those cool, disconcerting eyes dissected her. Then, 'I'll be the judge of that,' he stated bluntly, and she'd have given anything just then to have an ounce of his confidence. Especially when, brusque almost to the point of rudeness, he demanded, 'Do you want the job or not?'

God, she wouldn't want to get on the wrong side of him! But did she or did she not want the job? It was fast going from her mind what the job was, but she had always thought of herself as fairly confident and some spirit inside her was darned if she would turn within five minutes of knowing the man into someone who wished for an ounce of his. So, 'Yes, I want it,' she replied spiritedly, her chin tilting a defiant fraction as though to tell him in advance that it was no skin off her nose if he chose not to employ her valuable services.

Everything about her was noted, she was sure of that but, after pinning her with another cool look from his direct gaze, instead of telling her to collect her expenses on her way out as she fully expected, to her surprise he replied, 'Then I suggest we sit down and discuss it.'

Fabienne covered the unexpectedness of his reply by moving over to one of the several easy-chairs in the room and doing as he suggested. She observed that he did the same, and she busied herself crossing her ankles neatly while she waited for him to fire away with what—since the chosen applicant was going to be resident in his home—she was sure were going to be very pertinent questions indeed.

'Tell me about yourself, Miss Preston,' he invited with very little delay.

In her view that was hardly a job-interview-type question. 'What would you like to know?' she countered, and weathered his narrow-eyed look that indicated that if she was messing him about she'd get short shrift.

However, he must have decided to give her the benefit of the doubt, because he changed tack to enquire, 'Do you live at home or on your own?'

'I live with my family.'

'You're obviously happy living at home?'

'We're a very happy family.'

'But you want to leave?' He was in there like a flash, and left her gasping.

'This job *is* only temporary,' she bounced back, having got her second wind, not prepared to be intimidated by him or anybody else. 'I'm in between jobs at the moment and, since I'm not sure what sort of work I want to do in future, I thought a temporary job would give me space in which to decide.' That wasn't quite true but, as she thought about it, Fabienne realised that, since to work was in her genes, it was a very good idea.

'What sort of work have you been doing?'

'I've worked in a dress shop since I left school.'

'How old are you now?'

'Twenty-two.'

'Why did you leave the dress shop?'

That was easy. 'It closed down. But——' she smiled on an imp of mischief '—I can get a reference if you need one.' She wasn't going to get the job anyway, so there was little point in telling him that the gown shop had belonged to her mother.

She saw his glance on the sudden upward curve of her mouth, then those cool grey eyes were on hers again and he was asking, 'Have you ever had anything to do with children?'

'I've an eight-year-old nephew—we used to be great friends.'

'Used to be?' he took up.

'Philip's parents are divorced. We—um—don't see as much of him as we once did,' she explained quietly.

'Clearly you miss him?'

'I suppose I do,' she had to admit.

'Which, whether you know it or not, is probably the reason why you applied for the job of helping with a pair of seven-year-olds,' he decreed.

Had he studied under a disciple of Freud, for goodness' sake? She almost said as much, but only just then realised that there must be an invisible line between employer and employee which, because she'd always worked with her mother, she had never encountered. But it was one which it might be an idea to start learning about, so instead it seemed more politic to comment, 'You're probably right.' And, employer, employee, or not, she thought she had a right to ask one or two questions herself. 'Are the twins both boys?'

'One of each—Kitty and John.'

'They're at boarding-school?' she guessed, thinking that they must be coming home for the summer holidays—but knew she had guessed wrong when he shook his head.

'At the moment they're attending the village school about a mile from where I live.'

At the moment! Evidently Mr Tolladine was considering sending them elsewhere. 'And you're looking for someone to start—um—in July?' Fabienne asked, after a quick calculation of when the school term ended.

'They finish school towards the end of July,' her interviewer announced crisply after studying her for some moments. 'But——' he paused, his direct gaze taking in her fine features '—I should want the successful applicant to start more or less straight away.'

'To get to know the children first?' Fabienne queried, realising that he meant nothing of the sort. What he meant was that if—by some gross error of misjudgement—the person he decided upon did not suit, then that would give him ample time to dismiss her and find somebody else.

'Would you have any problem with that?' he queried in answer.

'None at all,' she replied. 'Er—what sort of duties would be expected of me—er—of the successful applicant?'

His look said he considered she should have known that before applying for the post but, oddly, she formed the impression that he was as vague about what a nanny-cum-mother's help did as she was. 'Take the children to school, meet them from school, generally make yourself useful—that sort of thing. You do drive?' he asked abruptly.

'I have my own car,' she answered, and thought it not impertinent in the circumstances to enquire, 'Does your wife follow her own career?'

'Wife?' he questioned, as though she had suddenly gone mad.

'M-Mrs Tolladine,' she stammered, feeling that he had wrong-footed her.

'There is no Mrs Tolladine.'

'No M——'

'I'm not married,' he declared, as though thinking that she was a little thick not to have cottoned on to that fact before.

'Well——' Fabienne bridled; it was all very well being clever when one was acquainted with all the answers, but no one had told her, until now, that there wasn't any Mrs Tolladine '—does your partner follow her own career?' she insisted. 'If the person you take on is to help the children's mother...'

'I have neither wife nor live-in lover,' her inquisitor fixed her with an arrogant look to state.

'Then who the blazes——?' Fabienne began spiritedly, but closed her mouth at his raised-eyebrow look. And knew then that she had just blown the interview.

She started to get to her feet and found he was on his feet, too—and that he was on his way to open the door. 'The children's mother,' he revealed, just before he opened it, 'is my sister-in-law. She's living in my home for a while.' And, totally unexpected when she just knew that she hadn't got the job, he handed her his personal card. 'I'll be in touch, Miss Preston,' he stated, and the next moment, his card in her hand, she was one side of the door and he the other.

She was still feeling slightly stunned at how abruptly her interview had ended, and was unsure which one of them had terminated the interview, when she became aware of Sonia Morris approaching her with an envelope. 'Your expenses, Miss Preston,' she began. 'I hope...'

'That's all right.' Fabienne smiled, waving the envelope away. 'I was coming to London today anyway.'

With that, she made her escape, and was heading downwards in the lift before she remembered the card she held. 'Vere Tolladine,' she read. 'Brackendale, Sutton Ash, Berkshire,' and his telephone number. Vere Tolladine? She knew that name from somewhere!

So intent was she on puzzling where she had heard the name of Vere Tolladine before that she was on a train on her way back to Oxford before she realised she had not carried out her intention to take a look around the shops. She rather thought that her interview with the Tolladine man was in part responsible for her forget-fulness, too—for never had she met a man anywhere near like him.

It was her father who gave the answer to where she had heard the name before. 'Vere Tolladine!' he ex-claimed as they sat around the dinner table that evening. 'Heavens, Fenne, surely you remember seeing him on TV the other week when sterling had a little hiccup. He's head of Tolladine Finance! He's always being quoted in the Press.'

Fabienne was positive that if she had seen Vere Tolladine before then by no chance would she have forgotten it. Though had to concede, for all she was not much into matters financial, that she must have seen his name in the papers from time to time.

She sat now in the car park of the George and thought of how ever since last Wednesday memory of that interview with Vere Tolladine had returned to haunt her. Leaving aside the many questions that darted in and out of her head, such as why was his sister-in-law living in his house? And was his brother living there too? He had to be, surely. For, if his brother had split from his wife, then it made more sense that he be the one to reside in Vere Tolladine's home. But, even as she pondered why he was taking such an interest, that he was the one doing the nanny-interviewing and not either of the children's parents, strangely, Fabienne could not seem to get him out of her mind.

That, she told herself logically, had to be because, in truth, she had never ever met a man quite like him. Though as she left her car and went into the hotel to meet her friends she acknowledged that when she had attended the job interview, completely unconcerned about getting it, something—some strange, nebulous, untouchable thing—had happened, during the interview and since that phone call tonight, that made her feel that she would not mind at all taking it on.

And now, thanks to that phone call, the job was hers! Was he, Vere Tolladine, conceivably right with his theoretical notion that she had applied for the job with children because she was missing the contact with her eight-year-old nephew?

Tomorrow she was due to move into the financier's house, so maybe she would find out. Although as she recalled those cool, direct grey eyes, not to mention his brusque attitude on the phone earlier, perhaps it was just as well that her weekly stint would be only Monday to Friday. With luck, he had a *pied-à-terre* in town and only came home to Sutton Ash at weekends.

CHAPTER TWO

SUNDAY dawned bright and clear, but when Fabienne went downstairs she found that her parents were having second thoughts about her moving out to take a live-in job—albeit only a Monday-to-Friday job.

'I'll be home again on Friday evening—Saturday morning at the latest,' she attempted to quieten their qualms about the youngest leaving their sheltered home.

'Perhaps I'll give Mr Tolladine a ring before you go,' her father terrified her by suggesting.

'*Daddy*!' she squeaked in alarm. 'How would you feel to have phone calls from the fathers of all the new females you employ?' She could see he was getting her point, and pressed on. 'Anyhow, you said yourself that his integrity is second to none, so I can't see that I shall come to any harm.'

She had never loved her father more when he gave her an ashamed grin, and muttered, 'So I'm an old fusspot.'

'A lovely old fusspot,' she laughed, and gave him a hug.

'What time will you be leaving?' her mother enquired.

That was a difficult one. No time had been mentioned but she doubted that—weekends being precious for anyone who must work as hard as Vere Tolladine—he would want her around interrupting his day of rest too early. 'Some time this evening, I think,' she replied.

'The children might be in bed by the time you get there,' her mother reminded her practically.

'That's all right; I can meet them in the morning.'

It was around seven-thirty that evening that Fabienne, with her case packed with enough clothes to last her a week, said goodbye to her parents and the dog Oliver, and steered her car in the direction of the next county.

She had thought it would take her an hour or so to reach Sutton Ash, but it was nearly two hours later that she found the village. Ten minutes later she found the house named Brackendale.

It was a large, sprawling two-storeyed house set in its own grounds, and Fabienne sailed up the long and winding drive realising that, though she had always thought of her family as being fairly well off, there was well off and again, very well off.

There was no one around and not a car in sight as she drew up near the front door and got out of her car. Since she was expected she took her case out of the boot and went and rang the front doorbell.

She did not have to wait long and, oddly, a bubble of excitement overtook her as she heard someone coming to answer the door. The person who answered the door, however, was not Vere Tolladine, but a tall, well-built lady of about fifty.

'I'm Fabienne Preston——' was as far as she got before the other woman broke into a welcoming smile.

'We're all ready for you. I'm Mrs Hobbs, the house-keeper,' she introduced herself. 'Come in. Come in.' Fabienne did as she was bid, taking to the friendly housekeeper at once. Then, as Mrs Hobbs went to close the door, she must have spotted her car. 'Ah—you'll want to park your car undercover overnight. Would you like to do it now, or later?'

'I might as well do it now,' Fabienne decided, and, leaving her case in the hall, was joined by Mrs Hobbs in her car and instructed where to steer it.

They went round to the rear of the house where there were several outbuildings and several garages. 'This one's for you,' the housekeeper stated and, the car safely put to bed for the night, she handed her the garage key and also a key to the rear door of the house. 'You'll need that some time, I expect,' she smiled, and as they crossed the yard she pointed out the lighted cottage in the grounds of Brackendale where she lived with her husband Sid, who worked as handyman about the property. 'You'll probably see Bob, the gardener, about the place tomorrow, too. Ingrid now comes to help out but, apart from Wendy, who comes up from the village every day to take charge of the cleaning, that's the lot of us,' she explained as she unlocked the rear door which led into a much smaller hall than the one at the main entrance.

They went in and she pointed out the breakfast-room, dining-room and the main drawing-room as they went through to the large black- and white-tiled entrance hall from which Fabienne saw the most elegant central staircase she had ever seen. She was still gazing at it in admiration when Mrs Hobbs, saying she would show her to her room, went to take a hold of her suitcase.

'I'll carry it,' Fabienne smiled, and just had to ask, 'Is Mr Tolladine, Mr Vere Tolladine around?'

'He's out, I'm afraid,' Mrs Hobbs replied.

Fine, thanks for the welcome, Fabienne thought, and promptly brought herself up short at the sour thought. Grief, he had better things to do than to sit at home waiting to welcome in the hired help. From what she remembered of the sophisticated look of him, he was probably out painting the town red somewhere with some equally sophisticated and chic female.

'Mrs Tolladine?' she enquired, thinking that she should perhaps make the acquaintance of the lady she was there to help.

'Mrs Tolladine?' the housekeeper queried as they reached the long, curving landing that had oak-panelled doors leading off in both directions.

'The children's mother?'

'Oh, you mean Mrs Hargreaves,' Mrs Hobbs caught on and, while Fabienne was wondering how come, if the children's mother was married to Vere Tolladine's brother, her name was Hargreaves, the housekeeper was saying, 'Mrs Hargreaves will introduce herself in the morning, I expect,' and was opening one of the doors along the landing and telling her, 'There's a bathroom adjoining, which separates you from the twins who are in the two rooms next to it.' And, as Fabienne took her suitcase into a high-ceilinged, elegant bedroom, 'Can I get you anything to eat or drink?' Mrs Hobbs enquired.

'Nothing, thanks,' Fabienne replied and, with the time turned ten o'clock by that time, 'I think I'll just unpack and get into bed.'

It did not take her long to unpack and to wash and get into bed. And, with a bed that was the last word in comfort, any thoughts that she might—since she was in a strange house and with people she barely knew—have difficulty sleeping were proved unfounded. For no sooner had she turned out her bedside light and closed her eyes than she fell fast asleep.

Some slight sound brought her awake. She opened her eyes to daylight and to the knowledge that she was not alone. For there, nightdress-clad and close to her bed, stood a very pretty blonde-haired child. 'Good morning.' Fabienne smiled encouragingly.

'Good morning,' the little girl responded. 'Are you the lady who's come to look after us?' she asked solemnly.

'Yes, I am,' Fabienne replied, aware that she must not rush to make friends but give the child space to go at her own pace. 'I arrived last night while you were asleep.'

'Uncle Vere said you'd be here this morning. My name's Kitty.'

She had just introduced herself when another sound caused Fabienne to look over to the door. There, clinging fearfully to the doorknob, she saw her other charge. He was dark-haired, like his uncle, but there any resemblance stopped. For his uncle was confident and sure of what he was about, whereas this small boy looked nervous and stood staring worriedly at her. 'Hello, come in,' she said gently, hoping to give him confidence.

Hesitantly, he moved just a little further into the room. He had melting blue eyes that Fabienne felt might melt into tears at any moment as they stared apprehensively at her.

'John's a bit shy,' his sister solemnly explained and, while Fabienne accepted that all children were different—some shy, some not—the solemn countenance of the one of her charges and the timidity of the other was something of a surprise, not to say shock. Without effort she recalled how boisterous her nephew Philip had been when, a year ago, he had been the same age as the twins. There had been no nervous entry into her bedroom when, after staying overnight with them as he occasionally had, he would hurl himself into her room and on to her bed ready and eager to start a new day.

She felt instinctively that she wanted to give the pair of them a cuddle, but she equally felt certain that it would be better if she let them find their own ground where she was concerned.

'I think I'd better get up,' she stated instead, but already the pair were on their way out of the room.

'Are you taking us to school please, miss?' Kitty turned to ask.

'I expect so,' Fabienne replied. 'Call me Fabienne.'

They went without another word and, while their general demeanour disturbed her slightly, she was not unduly worried until, showered and dressed in a short-sleeved collarless white linen shirt which she tucked into the belted waistband of a pair of white and pale green-striped trousers that suited her slim, long-legged figure, she left her room and found both children in one of the rooms along the landing which the housekeeper had pointed out as belonging to them the previous evening. Both children were dressed, after a fashion, and Kitty was rummaging around in a drawer for John's sweater. Where on earth was their mother? Their father for that matter?

'I expect you've had a wash,' she said calmly as the children suddenly became aware of her standing there.

'Sort of,' Kitty replied, pulling a sweater from a drawer with relief, and Fabienne made a mental note to have things organised better for tomorrow if, as seemed likely, neither of the children's parents were very good at getting up in the morning.

'What time do you have to be in school?' she asked, going over and rebuttoning John's shirt the right way up.

She didn't get an answer for just then Vere Tolladine, business-suited and every bit as good-looking as she remembered him, came into the room.

'You found us, then?' he greeted her, though she was sure he already knew of her arrival.

'I wasn't sure what time——' She broke off, realising from the hint she'd picked up from his tone that he'd expected her earlier. He had put her on the defensive. 'What time do we leave for school?' she asked instead.

Grief, what was it about this man? He didn't have to say a word of rebuke, and already she was bridling!

'Perhaps we should have breakfast first,' he drawled, and Fabienne could have hit him.

Mocking swine. Thank goodness she wouldn't have to see him for the rest of the day. He waited for them and the four of them went down the stairs together—she in front with his niece, he behind with his nephew who, so far, Fabienne had not heard utter a word.

Mrs Hobbs was bustling about the breakfast-room when they went in and she it was who—as though she did it every day—on this, Fabienne's first morning, attended to what the children wanted to eat.

This gave Fabienne the chance to ask her employer quietly, 'Bearing in mind I haven't done this sort of thing before, what shall I do today?'

'I'm sure you'll find something,' he replied, which in her view was not at all helpful. But, at her exasperated look, he condescended to suggest, 'Work something out with Rachel when you get back from taking the twins to school.' And before she could ask if Rachel was Mrs Hargreaves, his sister-in-law, he was asking, 'What sort of car do you have? Perhaps I should take a look at it before I go.'

From that she gathered that she was taking his nephew and niece nowhere if her car was some clapped-out deathtrap. 'Feel free,' she replied and, certain he had a duplicate garage key, 'It's parked in one of your garages,' she added. Her car was eighteen months old and in immaculate condition. 'Er—do you want to see my driving licence?' some imp of devilment pushed her to enquire.

For her sins she was favoured with a considering and raised-eyebrow look from her unamused employer. 'It would appear,' he murmured, 'that I made the right choice in selecting you to look after the children.' And searing hot colour scorched her skin.

'Thanks!' she huffed stiffly, not caring at all that he had just as good as told her that she was as childish as they had every right to be.

His eyes lingered on her flushed cheeks, he seemed about to say something, then appeared to change his mind, but there was a definite hint of an upward curve to his mouth when, 'You're quick, I'll give you that,' he told her. And, that hint of a smile sternly suppressed, he placed his napkin on the table and stood up, towering over her. 'Don't be late for school,' he instructed all three of them and, as something in Fabienne found that remark funny, and she discovered that she was the one who was sternly repressing a grin, he said goodbye to the twins, nodded in her general direction, and left them to it.

He was a pig, but he also had the ability to make her want to laugh. Fabienne was still trying to come to terms with the baffling mixture of the man, of how she reacted to the man, as she piled the children into her car and drove them to school.

Because of all the other cars parked there, Fabienne had to park the car some way away from the school gates. 'Come along, sweetheart.' She helped Kitty out first and, wanting John to leave the car on the pavement side, 'Not that door, love,' she told him gently when he tried to open the door on the road side.

With her two charges in tow, she walked with them to the school gates and, while exchanging smiles with the one or two 'mums' who stood there, she explained to both children why they must wait for her to open the car door for them. Neither of them said a word, and by then she was starting to wonder if John had a voice at all, for not so much as a peep had she heard out of him since she had lain eyes on him that morning.

Then she found that he did have a voice. She checked that they both had their lunch-boxes, which Mrs Hobbs had rushed out to the car for them—something which Fabienne admitted she hadn't given a thought to. Then, observing that there was a teacher in the playground generally keeping an eye on the children as they went in, she said goodbye to them and then saw that John appeared to have something on his mind.

'What is it, love?' she encouraged gently.

He stared at her from his lovely, moist and worried blue eyes, and then, in a voice that was husky with anxiety, said, 'Will you be here to meet us after school?'

Her heart went out to him. 'I certainly will,' she promised firmly, with a cheerful smile.

He did not smile back, but seemed satisfied and walked into the playground with his sister. He turned round once; Fabienne waved reassuringly. Still he didn't smile, but he did wave—and Fabienne found the strength of a maternal instinct in her so strong that she wanted to protect that little boy fiercely and personally slay all his dragons.

'You're new?'

Fabienne came away from her feelings about the young little chap she had only known for a few hours to find that a tall, lean man of about thirty had fallen into step with her. 'Who are you?' she enquired warily, not knowing if he was a parent or who he was, lurking by the school gates.

'Put your gun away,' he grinned. 'I've just brought my sister's kid to school. Name of Lyndon Davies, brilliant artist, only no one seems to have recognised it yet. Until they do, I'm living with my sister, name of Dilys Bragg, and in lieu of rent running her errands.'

Fabienne decided he was harmless and that she liked him. 'Fabienne Preston,' she replied.

'I saw you with the Hargreaves kids—are you related?'

Fabienne couldn't see what her relationship had got to do with him, but thought, since he could be the village gossip for all she knew, that she would prefer not to discuss the family she worked for with him.

'Let me put it another way,' he changed tack when there was no immediate answer forthcoming. 'Are you attached?'

She wanted to laugh—he wasn't the village gossip; he was the village flirt! She shook her head.

'Not even semi?' he pressed, as they reached her car and she halted by it.

'Not even semi,' she responded. My word, they were sharp in this neck of the woods.

'In that case, may I hope to show you the delights that Haychester restaurateurs have to offer one evening, as soon as you can make it?' And she just had to laugh.

Haychester, she knew from the map she had studied when checking out her route to Sutton Ash, was the nearest town about six or seven miles away. She opened her car door and prepared to get in behind the wheel. 'You may hope, Mr Davies,' she replied, 'but I think it's unlikely that——'

'Lyndon, please,' he requested.

She got into her car, closed the door and, giving him a friendly wave, she drove off. Most oddly, a minute or so later as she steered her car in the direction of Brackendale, Lyndon Davies was far from her mind and it was thoughts of Vere Tolladine that occupied her. He was, she suddenly realised, a most stimulating man. She had felt alive and on her toes at breakfast—even while having a few unpleasant names for him besides 'employer', she had felt charged, chirpy.

She was in the middle of wondering if they had breakfast with him every morning, or...when she caught herself up short. Good heavens, what on earth was she thinking about? She had more important things to be dealing with here than with that man who could make an insult sound like a compliment without you realising it—unless you were alert the whole time. Oh, how she wished she hadn't coloured up at his sardonic 'It would appear that I made the right choice in selecting you to look after the children'! Why she had, she would never know, for she hadn't blushed that she could remember in donkey's years. But—anyhow—she had more to think about than him. For a start, what were her duties this day?

She parked her car round the rear of the house in front of the garage that had been allocated to her. Since she'd be going out later to be at the school gates by ten past three there was little point in putting it away.

Fabienne entered the house by the rear door and hoped to run across Mrs Hargreaves, the lady she was there to assist, as she went from the smaller hall into the larger hall, up the exquisite staircase. She met no one but, thinking that perhaps she should attend to the children's laundry and tidy their rooms, she went first to the room she had been in earlier—John's room—and found her services were not required in that area.

An overall-clad young matron had the laundry all collected in a large plastic bag, and already had the bed made and the room straightened.

'Good morning—er—Ingrid,' Fabienne guessed. 'Is there anything I can help you with?'

'Oh, no, thanks, miss. I've done in here and the little girl's room. I give them a big turn-out on Thursday, but a dust and a tidy is all they usually need until then.'

Fabienne wandered back to her own room which she had tidied before breakfast. She did not want to be in the way, or slow anyone down by constantly asking if she could help in any way. They had their own Mrs Cooper back home who kept the house spick and span but who never minded if she occasionally lent a hand. But she had no wish to be thought intrusive.

Where, oh, where was Rachel Hargreaves? Should she go down and find Mrs Hobbs and ask her? It did not seem right, somehow, that she should do that. So for the next hour Fabienne stayed in her room with her ears forever on the listen for the sound of the mother she was here to help coming to find her and to ask for her assistance.

At half-past ten she went downstairs and into the drawing-room, of the view that, were it not for the sad expression on John Hargreaves' little face, she would be ready to throw in the towel on this workless job.

At five to eleven, just when she was thinking that, in the absence of anybody else, she would buttonhole her employer that evening—for tonight she was having second thoughts about hoping he'd got a *pied-à-terre* in town—and pin him down to exactly what her duties were, suddenly a plainly distressed woman, approaching thirty, opened the door and came in.

'I'm so sorry,' she apologised straight away. 'You must be Fabienne. I just...' Her voice started to tail off. 'I just—forgot.'

'That's all right.' Fabienne forgave her instantly when everything about the thin, brown-haired woman spoke of nothing being right with her world. It was all there in the hunted look of those anxious blue eyes, so like her son's.

'Did the children get off to school all right?' she asked and, in the same breath, 'Would you like coffee?'

'I can get some in a minute if you like,' Fabienne answered calmly. 'They're lovely children,' she added gently.

'They're so good. Not a moment's trouble. Although just lately the poor darlings——' She broke off and, clearly not wanting to pursue that line of her thoughts, she glanced out of the window, seemed to notice that it was a glorious sunny day. 'Would you like to go for a walk? I could show you around the grounds.'

'I'd love to,' Fabienne answered, and went to the door with her, doing a very rapid rethink on the duties of mother's help. Rachel Hargreaves needed help, certainly, but it wasn't the help in the kitchen or the housework kind of help that she needed, she was positive of that.

She seemed better once they were outside, however, and, seeming to have taken to the person her brother-in-law had engaged, she apologised again for being so late down, explaining that she had a bit of a sleeping problem and had taken a few sleeping-tablets.

Very strong ones, too, Fabienne thought, if they'd knocked her out until gone ten in the morning—though of course it could be that she had not taken them until the early hours, when she'd given in to the knowledge that if she didn't take a pill she just wasn't going to get any sleep at all.

'Think nothing of it,' she answered gently. 'The children and I had breakfast with Mr Tolladine, and then I drove them to school, and——'

'You didn't mind?'

'Driving them to school?'

'Mmm,' Rachel Hargreaves agreed and, to Fabienne's horror, seemed on the point of tears.

'Of course not,' she declared cheerfully, and wished she knew more about depression because, without having

picked up a medical book in her life, she felt sure that
depression of some sort was what Rachel Hargreaves was
suffering from. 'That's what I'm here for, to help you
wherever I can,' she added sincerely, all earlier notions
of but-for-John-Hargreaves-she-would-quit-this-non-job
flying as a great compassion for the woman took her—
she knew that she wanted to try and help if she could.

Which was why, when she was not an overly chatty
type of person, she chatted lightly about how pretty the
mile-long run to the school was, and how friendly the
mothers had seemed at the school gates. And, for good
light measure, she told her of how she had made the
acquaintance of Lyndon Davies and how, all in the space
of three minutes, he had asked her to go for a meal with
him some time.

'That,' she ended with a laugh, 'is fast! Though I
suppose there are men like that around who can't resist
trying to make a conquest at the——' Fabienne abruptly
broke off, again horrified when a strangled sort of cry
left Rachel Hargreaves and, as if everything was just too
much for her, she turned from her and went rushing back
to the house.

Fabienne's first instinct was to go rushing after her to
try to find out what the matter was. But she checked.
Somehow she had a feeling that something she had said
had upset her. That upset and worried Fabienne, too.
Then a light of determination suddenly lit her eyes. Until
she knew what went on here, she would for the moment
stay quiet. But find out what went on she most definitely
would.

Slowly she walked back to the house and went up to
the children's rooms to check on their wardrobes, making
sure that Kitty had a fresh dress for tomorrow and that
John had a fresh shirt, and everything else that they

would need. Tonight she would clean their shoes for to-morrow, but now to get back to today.

She went down to the kitchen where the motherly Mrs Hobbs greeted her warmly and asked if there was any-thing special she would like for lunch.

'A sandwich, or a bit of something on toast will be fine,' she answered and, with the notion in her head to take her main meal with the children, 'What time do Kitty and John eat?' she enquired.

'Unless Mr Tolladine's entertaining or has business people here, he dines early with the children. I think he wants them to feel wanted,' she confided, but, as if she felt she'd said a little too much, she hurried on, 'So, although they'll have a bit of a snack when they come in from school, Mr Tolladine tries to get home so they can all dine together at seven. You'll be dining with them, of course, Miss Preston.'

'Fabienne, please,' she smiled and, having learned what she wanted to know, and not wanting to give the housekeeper extra work, 'I can make my own sandwich,' she volunteered—and found that the smiling Mrs Hobbs wouldn't hear of it.

Fabienne saw not another sign of Rachel Hargreaves, and went to collect the children from school to be standing exactly where she had been standing when she'd said goodbye to Kitty and John. At a minute after three-fifteen John came tearing round the corner, looking for her.

He stopped the moment he saw her but she did not miss the look of relief on his face. Nor did she miss the shy way he put his hand in hers and held on to her as they waited for Kitty to join them.

'We usually have a drink and something to eat with Mrs Hobbs when we come home,' Kitty hinted as Fabienne drew up round the rear of Brackendale.

'Would you like to go and see her while I garage my car?'

'Come on, John,' Kitty pressed, and, the more keen of the two, she led him kitchenwards.

By the time Fabienne joined them they were seated at a massive kitchen table drinking freshly squeezed orange juice and tucking into home-made cake.

Afterwards they went upstairs and, while Fabienne went to investigate a room which Kitty told her was their playroom, the two children went off to see their mother.

They joined her in the playroom in next to no time, however. 'Mummy's having a lie-down,' Kitty told her solemnly. 'Can we watch TV?'

Things in this house were, to say the least of it, not normal, Fabienne mused. 'Yes, of course,' she smiled, turning to the set in the corner and tuning in to children's TV. Tomorrow she would organise matters a little differently. For today, there were a lot of questions buzzing around in her head—and one man whom she was hopeful to see at dinner that night to whom she would put some of those questions. In her view, it had been most unfair to throw her in at the deep end. The light of determination was in her eyes again. She wanted answers and tonight, even if he didn't come home and she had to ask Mrs Hobbs for his London phone number, she intended to have answers.

In the event she did not have to ask Mrs Hobbs for Vere Tolladine's telephone number, because he strolled into the dining-room about a minute after she had got the children seated.

Rachel Hargreaves was not down to dinner, she noted, as, fixing her with one of his direct looks, 'Perhaps you'd like to sit there, Fabienne,' he invited.

While he greeted the children and passed a few comments with them she took the chair he indicated, which turned out to be directly opposite his, she observed, when he too sat down.

In straight line of his vision, she refused to feel intimidated by his disconcerting gaze, but hardly knew where to begin when, with charm, he enquired politely, 'And how did your day go?'

Hardly with silver bells and cockleshells, and 'non-productive' sprang to mind, but there were children present. So, 'Fine,' she smiled, but, lest he should get complacent about that, 'Though if I could have a word with you later?'

She knew, or felt she knew, that he was the type of man who was of the 'if you've anything to say, then say it' school. But, for all she did not take to the sudden hard glint that came to his cool grey eyes, he was plainly aware that she did not want to discuss anything in front of the children, for he gave an almost imperceptible nod, and concentrated his attention on his nephew and niece.

It was going on for nine o'clock that night before she went to have that 'word' with him. By then she had supervised the children's baths, calmly sorted out any problems they had, tucked them up in bed with a kiss, and had generally cleared up everywhere.

She found Vere Tolladine in the drawing-room. He was nursing a Scotch. 'Drink?' he enquired, his tone affable, those 'miss nothing' eyes full on her.

She shook her head; she had more important matters on her mind. 'No, thanks,' she replied stiffly.

She saw one eyebrow ascend at her tone, though he did not refer to it but stated coolly, 'Then you'd better sit down and tell me what's stewing inside you. Or——' his eyes narrowed '—is it not going to take that long?'

Fabienne went and took a seat on one of the two comfortable couches in the room. With all she'd got queuing up to be asked, she might be here all night. He shrugged—clearly he got the message.

'Fire away,' he invited.

She wished he would sit down. He was making her feel—exposed, somehow. Rot! stated that determined streak, and she fired away—from both hips. 'You deceived me!' she stated hotly—oh, grief, she sounded like some Victorian maiden.

If he thought so too, however, she was grateful that he did not say as much, but fired bluntly back, 'How?'

'At interview—when I came to see you in London— you deceived me into thinking——'

'And what about the deception you played on me?' He chopped her off before she could get up a full head of steam.

'What deception?' she demanded. Really, he was the end!

'The deception that you needed a job in the first place!'

Trust him to turn the attack on her! 'You checked me out!' she exclaimed as the penny dropped.

'Did you think I'd let anyone loose with a couple of vulnerable children without first——?'

'Talking of vulnerable children——' she attempted to get in.

'I know that your father owns a thriving and well-thought-of engineering company, and that you did not merely work in a "dress" shop, but that your family owned one of the best women's outfitters in Lintham.' He chopped her off, paused, and then, his direct look piercing hers, clearly remembering the way she had told him at that interview that she could get a reference if she needed one, 'Did you intend to write your own reference?' he asked.

He'd got her there. 'It would have been a good one,' she replied, and just had to grin. She saw his lips twitch as if her pert reply had tickled his sense of humour. But his eyes were on her impish mouth and suddenly he was looking serious again. And that was when Fabienne woke up—grief, where was her head? There were serious things to be discussed here! 'So, you having accepted me for the job, and having just completed my first day in the job, I have to tell you that——'

'You want to leave?' he barked aggressively.

Heaven help us, where was the man who had almost smiled a moment ago? 'Are you asking me to leave?' she returned spiritedly.

She'd heard of a Mexican stand-off, and wondered if this was it. For, as he stared hostilely at her, so she stared hostilely at him. 'I'd prefer not to go through that interview rigmarole again,' he drawled, after some moments.

Fabienne wasn't fooled. Since it was only last Wednesday that the interviews had taken place, he would still have names and addresses of the other interviewees on file, and could quite easily contact his second choice. However, since it seemed he was not asking her to leave, she felt it better that she get down to the root of why she had asked to see him.

She flicked a glance over to the fireplace where he stood, and waited only while he placed his glass down upon the mantel to launch in with, 'As you know, when I applied for this job I'd no idea of what a nanny-cum-mother's help did. I suppose I imagined I'd be doing something like sewing buttons on the children's clothes, helping with the laundry, some bits of housework but, apart from chauffeuring the twins to and from school, checking out their wardrobes and supervising bathtime, I've done nothing today!'

'You're complaining because you haven't enough to do?' he enquired sardonically.

She hated him—and the gloves came off. 'I'm complaining because you should have told me that the woman I'm here to assist is as near to a nervous breakdown as dammit, and——'

'When did you qualify as a psychiatrist?'

God—what was it about this man that made her alternately want to laugh or thump him? 'I don't need to be a psychiatrist to see that Mrs Hargreaves is deeply depressed.'

'You've obviously met her?'

'This morning—briefly,' Fabienne acknowledged.

'It worries you that she's—a bit down?'

A bit down! 'Of course it does!' she replied heatedly. Grief, what did he think she was that she could see the way his sister-in-law was and not feel for her?

'But—you don't want to leave?'

'I'm worried for her—*not* for me!' she erupted, realising that they had been at cross purposes. But, before he could get all shirty at her tone, Fabienne rushed on. 'I said my meeting with Mrs Hargreaves was brief——' She halted. 'Why is your sister-in-law Mrs Hargreaves and not Mrs Tolladine?' she questioned.

To her relief, he left his place over by the mantel and took his ease on the couch opposite. 'You haven't asked around?' She gave him a speaking look which she hoped conveyed that she had more about her than that, and did not deign to answer. 'My God, there's enough side on you——' he began shortly, but checked and, it seemed, decided in view of her show of loyalty—that she hadn't asked the staff what she wanted to know—to give her a few answers. 'Rachel,' he stated quietly, 'was married to my stepbrother.'

'So she's your stepsister-in-law.' Fabienne quickly filed that away. 'She's divorced from your stepbrother?' she queried as that 'was' sank in. 'Forgive me for asking, but I'm not asking out of idle curiosity.' She went on, 'Unthinkingly—and without knowing how—I said something this morning that inadvertently caused her pain.'

'You did?' he questioned seriously, the whole of him alert-sharp.

Fabienne nodded. 'We were walking in the garden— just chatting—then she took off, clearly upset, and I haven't seen her since. She didn't come down to dinner, and...'

'Mrs Hobbs took a tray to her room,' Vere stated, as if he knew it for fact, and Fabienne silently thanked him for telling her that. Maybe he had accepted that she was worried for his stepsister-in-law and not for herself. 'Can you remember what you were talking about—at the time that Rachel took off?'

'It was nothing of any consequence,' she admitted, and owned, 'I could see that Mrs Hargreaves was feeling low so, more to try and cheer her up than anything, I rattled inconsequentially on and mentioned some man I'd met at the school gates who, within three minutes of meeting, had asked me for a date, and——'

'The devil he did!' her employer exploded.

'It happens.' She shrugged, and felt the most peculiar tingly feeling take her when Vere Tolladine studied her dainty features, her olive-tinted complexion and her shining, long black hair for some long seconds.

She didn't know quite how she felt when, 'With you,' he commented, his eyes still on her, 'I rather expect it does.' But that was definitely a compliment, wasn't it? Although with him, she guessed, one could never be sure.

'Anyhow,' she resumed, 'I was still trying to cheer Mrs Hargreaves when I said something about it being fast—all that happening in the space of three minutes—and something about some men not being able to resist trying to make a conquest, when she just left me, and went hurrying back to the house. It's plain that I said something that upset her,' Fabienne went on, 'which is why I've been afraid to seek her out for the rest of the day in case I inadvertently again said something that desperately hit a nerve.'

'So you decided to see me at the first opportunity so that I might tell you areas of conversation which it might, perhaps, be better to avoid?'

'I need to know a lot more than I do,' Fabienne stated. 'Though if Mrs Hargreaves is divorced from her husband, then——' She hesitated. Stepbrothers or no, they could quite well be as close as blood brothers and it just didn't seem fair to state what her intelligence had brought her—that Vere Tolladine's stepbrother must be a man with an eye for the ladies.

'In point of fact,' Vere took up, 'Nick and Rachel were not divorced.'

'Oh!' she exclaimed. 'Were?' she queried, picking up his use of the past tense again.

For long seconds he eyed her steadily then, his expression stern, he filled in that blank for her by revealing, 'My stepbrother was killed in a car crash last November.'

'Oh, no!' she whispered, her soft heart going out to Nick Hargreaves' widow, the twins and his stepbrother. 'Oh, I'm sorry,' she murmured sympathetically. No wonder Rachel was depressed! She had more to be depressed about than Fabienne had realised!

Just then, though, she became aware of Vere looking at the compassion in her eyes, and her sensitivities were pulled all ways when he quietly further informed her, 'Perhaps, to prevent any more upsets, I should explain that my stepbrother was not alone in the car at the time of the crash.'

Fabienne flicked her glance momentarily away from his. She was not stupid, but was again afraid of hurting his feelings. 'A woman?' she queried, glancing to him again. He nodded, leaving it to her to work it out. 'He was having an affair?' she guessed again, and again he nodded. 'One—of many?' she questioned slowly.

'He liked,' Vere stated emotionlessly, 'to make conquests.'

Oh, God! And she'd rushed in with both feet. His poor wife! 'Is there anything else I should know?' she asked huskily.

'I think that about covers it.'

Fabienne stood up, and so did he. She wanted to say something, anything, but she felt choked—and what was there that she could say? 'Then I'll—say goodnight,' she murmured.

She went swiftly from the room, conscious that her emotions were showing, conscious of his eyes on her as she went. She climbed the stairs and went to bed. She had more than enough to think about.

CHAPTER THREE

BY WEDNESDAY Fabienne had been in Rachel Hargreaves' company sufficient for them to be on first-name terms, but Rachel was otherwise very withdrawn and quiet. For Fabienne on the plus side, although he wasn't any more talkative than he had been, John seemed to be following his sister's lead and appeared to be on the way to trusting her. His large blue eyes had followed her round the room last night when, as he lay tucked up in his bed, she'd pottered about his room tidying up.

'Fabienne,' he'd called.

'Yes, love,' she'd answered.

He had swallowed painfully. 'Will you still be here in the morning?' he'd asked, in that husky little voice of his, and her heart cried for him. Poor little scrap, he wasn't certain of anything any more—one moment his father whom he'd loved had been there, and the next—not.

'You bet I'll be here,' she had smiled, and didn't think it would hurt a jot if she went and gave him an extra cuddle.

On the minus side, she found Vere Tolladine very confusing. She remembered how on Monday night she had thought he had dropped a compliment her way, but how last night, over dinner, he had barely seemed to glance her way. True, Rachel had been at dinner and he had given a lot of attention over to her and—— Fabienne stopped mid-thought. Ye gods! The thought rushed in from nowhere. Was she jealous?

Of course I'm not. She tossed that absurd notion out from where it came and, at dinner that night, was happy to assure herself that she did not have a jealous bone in her body and that since Rachel was so quiet, and was having such a tough time of it, it was no wonder that Vere should take time to try to draw her out.

It went without saying that he was fully aware that one Fabienne Preston needed no drawing out, and was fully able to take care of herself, thank you very much. With such thoughts in her head there was only one answer she could make when, as dinner ended and they began to leave the dining-room—Rachel a little ahead with the children—Vere looked down at her and questioned urbanely, 'Any more problems?'

Was he being solicitous or sarcastic? She did not give him the benefit of the doubt. 'Not one,' she replied loftily, flicked him a glance, saw the way he frowned down on her, and went speedily forward to catch up with the children. She was aware of Vere's eyes boring into her back, though, and didn't know who was comforting whom when she felt John timidly slide his little hand into hers. Hand in hand they went up the stairs together.

To Fabienne's surprise and pleasure, Rachel was up early the next morning. Between them they got the children ready for school, and all four of them went down to breakfast together.

If Vere was surprised to see Rachel downstairs at that hour, too—for it was the first time that week that it had happened—he gave no sign but asked, as they got the twins' breakfast requirements under way, what plans they had for the day.

Rachel looked blank, plainly not having thought beyond the effort of getting up that morning. 'I wouldn't mind taking a look round Haychester, actually,' Fabienne remarked off the top of her head and, turning to Rachel,

'Do you think we could go? We could be back ages before school comes out.'

'Ooh, if you're going to Haychester, can I have some of those pink socks I told you about?' Kitty got in quickly.

'What have you done?' Rachel turned to Fabienne and seemed to be on the point of smiling as she remarked, 'My daughter has the most appalling taste—she'll be wearing fluorescent pink socks to go to bed in if we don't watch her.'

'Perhaps bed is the best place to wear them,' Fabienne laughed—and turned her head in time to see that Vere Tolladine had his eyes fixed on no one but her.

It disturbed her. And annoyed her. And she was still both disturbed and annoyed that, when she had better things to think about, he was still in her head as, after dropping the children off at school, she and Rachel drove into Haychester.

They took a look around the shops but, save for picking up a pair of—it had to be admitted—hideous and fiercely pink socks for Kitty and a small modelling kit for John, they made no other purchases. Rachel had declined the suggestion that they have coffee in town, and was a silent passenger as Fabienne drove back to Sutton Ash.

Though as they turned into the gates of Brackendale and started up the drive it was Rachel, on observing that a car had just pulled up by the front door, who remarked, 'It looks as though we have a visitor!'

Fabienne recognised the car before its tall, fair-haired occupant got out. A smile was already on her face as, hearing the car engine, the man turned and, recognising her car, came towards them.

'Alex!' Fabienne squealed as she left her car and was enfolded in her brother's bear hug.

'*Konnichiwa*!' he grinned, having been in Japan on business for the past month and plainly having picked up an odd word or two.

'Show-off!' she laughed, and asked excitedly, 'When did you get back?' She did not get an immediate answer for just then Alex saw what she had forgotten—that she was not alone. 'Oh, Rachel, come and say hello to my big brother,' Fabienne included her quiet companion straight away. 'Alex has been out of the country for some weeks and...'

But Alex was already shaking hands with Rachel, and Rachel was inviting him indoors. And to Fabienne's surprise was remarking, 'You won't want to dash off if it's some time since you've seen your sister. Can you stay to lunch?'

'Afraid not,' he declined. 'I've one or two people to see this afternoon, but since I was this way...'

Alex worked in the capacity of sales director but every so often he liked to get out and chat personally to some of their valued customers. Fabienne couldn't help but feel a glow that he had lost none of his brotherly caring. He was still keeping an eye out for her and, quite plainly, he wanted to see for himself that she fared well in her new job—albeit temporary.

'Would you like coffee?' Rachel asked as they entered the drawing-room, and Fabienne, who was amazed and delighted that Rachel had been able to hide her depression as her excellent manners came to the fore, felt that the other woman was planning to do a disappearing act any minute now.

So, 'Of course you would,' she chipped in. 'I'll go and see Mrs Hobbs. Coffee for three won't take a minute.'

With Mrs Hobbs up to her elbows in flour, Fabienne made the coffee herself, plus one for the housekeeper, and hurried back to the drawing-room to note, with relief, that Rachel was still there.

Alex did not stay long, but Fabienne felt a terrific sense of achievement that Rachel remained with them right up until the moment that Alex stood up to go. Fabienne went out on to the drive with him and, as expected, heard him ask, 'What in creation made you take this kind of a job?'

'Confucius he say, a change...'

'...is as good as a rest,' Alex finished for her, and asked seriously, 'You're all right here, Fenne?'

'Who wouldn't be?' she laughed, but could see he wanted a serious answer. 'Yes, I'm fine. Rachel's quiet, but very nice. She—um—lost her husband last year, and...'

'So she said,' Alex replied solemnly, and asked, 'It's still only temporary, then, this job?'

Fabienne realised that her parents had told him all there was to tell. 'It's only for the school summer holidays,' she confirmed.

'What about when Rachel returns to her own home? She'll probably need——'

'Her own home?' Fabienne queried. While comprehending that Alex had seen that Rachel was not well, somehow she had never given thought to Rachel's living anywhere but Brackendale. 'I didn't know...'

Alex gave her a superior-brother grin. 'You haven't been asking the right questions, kid,' he teased. Then, giving a quick glance to his watch, 'See you,' he stated, gave her a hug and kiss, and went on his way.

Fabienne went back indoors, wondering that she had just assumed that Rachel had always lived at Brackendale with her husband and children, when it was much more natural that she and her family would have a home of their own.

Not that it was important in any way other than to make her realise that Vere must have invited Rachel to stay for a while after the death of his stepbrother.

Rachel had disappeared from the drawing-room when Fabienne returned. She guessed that she had gone up to her room, but Fabienne was not downhearted about that. In her view it had been a great step forward that she had got her out of the house at all that morning. And the way Rachel's inbred good manners had surfaced over how dreadful she must be feeling when Alex had been there was another bonus. As, too, was the fact that Alex—no doubt by the gentle probing that would be his way—had been able to get her talking. She doubted that Rachel had volunteered the information that she was widowed, but it said a lot for Alex's kindness of manner that he'd got her to open up sufficiently to reveal that much—and more.

Rachel was still in her room when it came time to go and collect the children. Fabienne decided, as 'mother's help' took on a new meaning, not to push her luck with helping Rachel through her depression any more that day. So, instead of knocking on her door and asking her to come with her, she went alone to the school.

She was much heartened, though, when Rachel joined her and the children as they went down to dinner.

Vere was already in the dining-room and Fabienne saw his glance encompass them all as they went in and took their places at the dinner table. Had he noticed that Rachel had found sufficient will to wash her hair at some time that afternoon? she wondered. Did he see that she was making every effort she could? That she had even bothered to put on a little make-up?

There was little he missed, she realised a moment later. 'I see you made it into Haychester,' he looked directly at Fabienne to remark.

She was intrigued. 'How do you know that?'

He shrugged and, with a glance to Kitty, whose feet were tucked under the table well out of sight, 'How else? My pretty little niece, here, is wearing a pair of socks the pink of which I would swear I've never seen before.'

Kitty chuckled in delight, and Fabienne stifled a laugh. Her mild suggestion that another shade of sock might go better with her purple frock had met with a tearful expression, so she had not pressed it. Fabienne could do nothing about the merriment that lit her eyes, though. Eyes that all at once linked with cool grey eyes that held hers and which, to her mind, did not look cool at all.

A moment later Vere took his glance from her to engage Rachel in conversation, and Fabienne was scoffing at any notion that there had been any warm look in his eyes. There was a warmer look in his eyes now, admittedly, but that was for Rachel, and not for her.

Her breath suddenly and unexpectedly caught. Was that warm look in his eyes for his stepsister-in-law warm-encouraging, or warm—er—personal? With something of a jolt, Fabienne realised that she did not care for that last thought at all. She was never more glad than when the meal came to an end and she was able to leave the dining-room.

She was going along the hall to the stairs when she heard a phone ringing and Vere went to answer it. She and Rachel were ambling past the study door, the children already halfway up the stairs, when Vere came from his study.

'There's a call for you,' he announced. Fabienne looked to Rachel, but Rachel was walking on. 'For *you!*' Vere clipped.

'Me!' she murmured, startled, and was nonplussed for the moment—as much by the impatient look on her employer's face as anything. 'Shall I...?'

'Take it in here,' he instructed, and stood to one side.

Fabienne entered the large, businesslike study musing on how she had given her parents this number but had not thought that they would use it. Particularly now that Alex had paid her a visit and had no doubt reported back that they had nothing to worry about. Besides, she would be seeing them at the weekend!

She picked up the phone. 'Hello,' she said, and discovered that it was neither of her parents, but her old friend Tom Walton.

'Hi!' he answered. 'I rang your home quite forgetting you'd said on Saturday that you were starting a Monday-to-Friday job in darkest Berkshire this week. Your mother gave me your phone number—how's it going?'

'Great!' she replied enthusiastically, even with her back to the door very much aware of Vere Tolladine somewhere in the vicinity. 'Er—I'm just about to read the children a bedtime story, actually,' she hinted.

'In other words, I haven't got time for a chat so goodbye until Saturday, Tom Walton.'

She had to laugh. 'Saturday?' she queried.

'I knew I was right to ring to give you a reminder. We're playing boule and you're in my team.'

'Can't wait!' she laughed.

She still had a pleased smile on her mouth when a minute or so later she ended the call and turned, to find Vere standing not two yards away.

A little taken aback—clearly he must have been listening to her every word—she stared at him. And just could not believe her ears when, 'Who was that?' he enquired tersely.

'A friend!' she replied, her tone equally terse, and saw his lips compress.

'Boyfriend?' he gritted.

Good grief, if he'd said 'no male callers'—not that Tom Walton was a 'caller'—she would not have been surprised, for that was what his expression clearly said. 'Of that gender,' she retorted sniffily and, uncaring that he appeared to care for neither her tone nor the fact that she might have a boyfriend, she went past him. Talk about Middle Ages, she fumed.

By morning Fabienne had cooled down enough to be able to see that it was perhaps not the fact that she might have a boyfriend that had made Vere so disgruntled-looking, but that he was concerned to guard the twins. He was a wealthy man, so the security of anyone living in his home was paramount. Look at how quickly he'd had her checked out before inviting her to come and help with a pair of vulnerable children. It was obvious to her then that, since she and her background had checked out OK, it followed that he would need to know more details of any male friend who might take it into his head to pay her a visit.

Fabienne had just decided that she had been an idiot not to have seen all this the night before when—very, very quietly—her bedroom door began to open, and a moment later John—shy, timid, and so very unsure of himself—stood there.

'Hello, treasure.' She greeted him with a smile and, because her heart ached for him, 'Got a hug for me?' she asked.

In a second he had run over to her. She leaned over and put her arms around him, and he gave her a tight but swift hug, and as wordlessly as he'd come in he went out again, quietly closing the door after him.

She had been here less than five days, she reflected, but already both the children had taken over a part of her heart. For, even though she tried to be so grown-up, Fabienne had caught Kitty so many times looking lost and sad, just like her twin.

Fabienne determined as she got out of bed that she was going to do everything in her power to give the twins more confidence and all she could to take some of the sadness out of their little faces.

In such determined mood she got them washed and school-uniformed and, aware by now that Rachel might surface only when the effects of her sleeping-pill had worn off, she took the children down to breakfast.

Vere lowered his newspaper as they entered the breakfast-room. 'Good morning.' Fabienne added her pleasant greeting to that of the twins—she was going to be pleasant in front of them, even if it killed her.

But she found that she had no need to pretend a pleasantness when, a hint of a smile touching his mouth, Vere looked from the twins and rested his cool grey eyes on her. Still with his eyes on her—those eyes straying to her shiny, long black hair and back to her large brown eyes again—'Good morning, you three,' he answered genially. As the children took their places at the table and she too sat down, Fabienne could not help but wonder what it was about this man that his mood could—or should—so affect her own mood.

She shrugged such unfathomable thoughts away and concentrated on the children's breakfast needs. Which did not take long because all either of them wanted was a small bowl of cereal, which they disposed of while their uncle asked them various questions about what lessons they were scheduled to do that day.

He's kind, she couldn't help thinking. Well, he is to them, she qualified as she stared at the firmness of his jaw, that strength in his face that said while he might be kind to children and dumb animals, cross him and you would see a very different side of him. Without a doubt Fabienne knew that, if he had to be, he could be ruthless.

Her eyes went to his and as their eyes met, so a sudden flush of colour stained her face—he had been watching her watching him! Hurriedly she glanced to see that both the children had taken all the breakfast they wanted. Damn him, damn him to hell, she thought in quite some confusion. She *never* blushed, yet twice she had done it with him there to see.

'Kitty, John, why don't you both go and see if Mrs Hobbs has your lunches packed ready for you?' she suggested as she fought desperately to get herself under control. What *was* it about this man? 'You know Mrs Hobbs likes to see you before you go off for the day.'

Like the darlings they most often were they obediently trotted off and, having engineered the minute of private conversation she needed with her employer, Fabienne found herself pinned by his waiting look that plainly asked, since she had gone to the kitchen with the children for the last three mornings, what she had on her mind.

Fabienne wasted not another moment but wished Vere had not caught her making a study of him, nor witnessed that cursed blush. It made her feel awkward when she had no need to. 'I was wondering,' she spoke up, 'does my weekend off start on Friday night or Saturday morning?' Oh, crumbs, she didn't like the sudden look of hostility that came to his face.

'Weekend off?'

Grief, you'd think it was all news to him! 'We never—er—actually got around to discussing it.' She stayed in there, determined not to be put off by his attitude.

'Hrmph!' he grunted and, giving her the full blast of a piercing grey look, 'Last night's phone-call has nothing to do with your sudden desire to rush off?' he snarled.

God give her strength, she prayed, as that sensation of wanting to thump him one took her again. 'I've a date tomorrow, if you could call it that,' she concurred sweetly. 'But the advert you put in the paper said weekends off. I merely want to know if I——'

'You *do* intend to come back?' he grated.

'Who could keep away?' she retaliated, and was on the receiving end of what she considered to be a most murderous look before Vere Tolladine angrily got up from the table.

She was angry, too, but was in no way prepared for his curt, blunt and—to her mind—most nasty and un-called-for, 'Go when the hell you like!' as he strode from the room.

Swine! Perfect pig of a man! she fumed—then in a flash had the whole of her anger negated when a sound alerted her to the fact that she had company, and she turned to see a worried-looking John standing there.

'Are you going to come back, Fabienne?' he asked, his gorgeous blue eyes on the brink of shedding tears, she could tell.

'Oh, darling, of course I am,' she crooned, going over to him and putting her arms around him.

It was on John's account that later that morning Fabienne rang her mother and told her not to expect her until the next day. So much for her determination to do all she could to boost the twins' confidence. Quite patently, little John had overheard enough of her conversation with his uncle to have his confidence that she would be there for him once the weekend was over shattered.

In contrast to the day before, Fabienne found that Rachel was having such a down day that even to so much as leave her room was an effort. Which made it just as well that she was there for the children, Fabienne realised, for, having presented herself early at the school gates— and run the gauntlet of Lyndon Davies again trying to get her to go out to dinner with him—Fabienne found that, when she took the children to dinner that night, they had the dining-room to themselves.

'Uncle Vere's probably meeting a lady,' Kitty opined, her mother's absence accepted without reference.

'I expect he is,' Fabienne smiled—but oddly found she had never felt less like smiling.

To her mind, Vere was still a swine. Though she felt she had enough evidence of his feelings of responsibility where the children were concerned to know that he must have covered the eventuality of neither her, nor Rachel, nor himself being there for dinner that night. No doubt Mrs Hobbs would have given the children their evening meal in her neat but cosy kitchen.

Fabienne continued to supervise the children after dinner, and went with them, too, when they went to say goodnight to their mother. 'Anything I can do to help?' she stayed to whisper to Rachel as the twins left her. Rachel's eyes were red-rimmed and she was all too obviously having a bad time of it. Rachel shook her head. 'I can come back and chat, play cards, anything you like?' she tried again.

'Please, no. Leave me,' Rachel answered.

'Are you sure?'

'I'm sure. It's—I'm...I'll take a pill soon and have an early night.' Rachel did her best to smile as she looked at Fabienne's concerned expression. 'Don't worry. Although it may not seem like it, I care too much about

Kitty and John—not to mention myself—to take more than the prescribed dose.'

With that Fabienne had to be satisfied, and she had to leave her, feeling saddened that yesterday Rachel had seemed to be making a little progress. She pinned a bright smile on her face and went into the playroom where the children were making a half-hearted attempt to tidy up the paints they had been using after school.

'I'll do that later!' she declared cheerfully. 'Now, who's first for a story tonight?'

Fabienne finally went to her own bed in a restless frame of mind. She found she could not sleep and sat up in bed again, put on the light and tried to immerse herself in her paperback. But she could not settle. On the one hand thoughts of John and how he had seemed more anxious than ever bothered her. On the other— was Vere Tolladine coming home tonight, or wasn't he? Not that she cared, but...

She tossed him irritatedly out of her mind and dwelt on young John, again feeling that his overhearing some of her conversation with his uncle that morning might have quite a lot to do with his present state of anxiety.

With her limited knowledge of children it seemed to her that, having lost his father, stability in his young life was what the little boy needed. He had taken to her, it seemed, appeared to be trusting her more and more each day. But, thanks to overhearing his uncle's 'You *do* intend to come back?' that morning, the poor little scrap was taking some reassuring.

Impatiently, Vere Tolladine back in her head again, she put down her book and put out her light. Damn the wretched man, she fumed, and tried for sleep. It was all his fault.

Fabienne fell into a kind of surface sleep with dark, unhappy shapes and images in her head. Something awakened her, and at first she thought she was still asleep. Then she heard a cry, a distressed shout—and she was out of bed like a shot.

On winged feet she went flying down the landing, illuminated by one wall-light left on in a far corner, and knew, even before that cry came again, which room that sound had come from. In a flash she had the door open and was in John's room. He was awake and much distressed.

In moments she was over by his bed, sitting on the edge of it, an arm around his shoulders. 'What's the matter, darling?' she crooned softly, her face close to his in the dim glow of his nightlight as she looked into his deeply troubled, tear-drenched eyes.

'I w-was falling over,' he hiccuped shakenly.

'You've had a bit of a bad dream, that's all,' she soothed, though 'ghastly nightmare' seemed more aptly to cover it, she thought, and was in the middle of giving him a comforting cuddle when she realised they had company.

'Is this a private party or can anyone join in?' Vere queried in a low tone.

Fabienne looked up to the shirt- and trouser-clad man who was now moving a chair near to the bed, and unexpectedly she felt her heart start to pound. 'John had a nasty dream,' she replied. 'What time is it?' Now why had she asked that?

'Around two,' he replied.

And he'd just got in! For goodness' sake—she pulled herself together. It was Friday night! What did she expect? That a man who worked as hard as he must would not play equally hard? She put her mind to finer things. 'Do you know where the kitchen is?' she questioned as John, no longer crying, snuggled up against her.

Vere favoured her with a raised-eyebrow look. 'Did I volunteer for something?'

He caught on quickly. 'One of us wants to make a small glass of warm milk.'

'Then I'm sure it must be me,' he drawled, and left his chair, leaned over to ruffle his nephew's hair gently, and ambled out.

For all he did not seem to hurry he was back, with a glass of warmed milk, in no time—and John was nodding drowsily. How to tell him he'd had a wasted journey? There was no need. As ever quick to catch on, Vere took one glance at the now comforted youngster and, without more ado, drank the milk.

And Fabienne, all at once more light-hearted than she had felt for quite some hours, was hard put to it not to burst out laughing. Fear that she might disturb the almost-asleep boy if laughing made her body shake stopped her, and she gently eased him down the bed, placed a light kiss on his brow and let go her hold on him.

She straightened up and only then, as she caught Vere's eyes on her, did she realise that, where he was dressed, she had dashed out of bed in such a rush that she was clad only in a thin cotton nightie. She saw his eyes move to her dark, all-anyhow hair and wished she had grabbed up a robe with one hand in passing, and a comb with the other.

She felt embarrassed suddenly, and was relieved when a hasty look at John showed that his eyelids were still closed and that his breathing had evened out to be regular and was that of a sleeping child.

Fabienne felt that she could safely leave him and went silently from the room—and found that Vere was right there with her.

'Shall we leave his door open?' he enquired softly, and while she warmed to him for his understanding, she also realised that he knew less about children than she did.

She nodded and saw that, while possibly he had not had so much to do with children as the little she had, there must be a very fine sense of responsibility in the man, quite a depth of sensitivity, that he should house them under his roof.

They reached her room before his—she saw an open door some way along the semi-circular landing which must be his—and she turned, intending to offer a swift goodnight.

But suddenly the word got stuck in her throat and could not be said. For Vere was looking at her, his look warmer for her than she had ever seen it, and something—something she could not give a name to just then—stirred in her for him.

She saw him scrutinise her face, saw the half-smile that came to his mouth—his quite extraordinarily good-looking mouth, she realised—then his glance went to her hair, to her scarcely clad body where the round contours of her breasts pushed at the cotton material of her nightdress.

And then, his tone sounding as husky as that of his nephew, '*Did* I choose right, to choose you?' he asked, and Fabienne was not sure just then if he was asking her, or himself.

'Don't doubt it,' she replied, and was somehow un-surprised that her voice was husky, too. She smiled gently, because that was how she felt. Gentle and tender—and at this time of the night, with her small charge gently seen to and tenderly sleeping, to introduce a cool note would be an intrusion.

She saw Vere's eyes go to her mouth—and linger there. Felt his imperceptible movement towards her. But then he checked, if indeed it had not been in her imagination anyway.

But abruptly he took his gaze from her slightly parted lips and, 'Goodnight, Fabienne,' he bade her, and moved away.

Swiftly she went into her room. She had been unable to answer him. Unable because never in her life, without so much as his laying a finger on her, had she felt such an undercurrent of electricity pass between her and any male. Never had she been so aware of anyone. Had he kissed her, she knew she would have kissed him back.

CHAPTER FOUR

IT WAS a blessing, Fabienne felt, that with the coming of daylight came sanity. She was up much earlier than usual, and showered, shampooed her hair and donned her robe to sit by the window looking out at the tranquil view of lush green meadows, trees and hedgerows—Vere Tolladine on her mind.

She was more able then to rationalise than she had been some hours previously. By then she was able to see far more clearly that of course she had never been so aware of any man as she had been of him. Never before, at gone two in the morning, had she stood in such thin cotton covering while some cool, good-looking sophisticate had stared down at her—and her scantily clad form! She felt the heat rush to her cheeks just to remember it.

Fortunately, at that point, her door opened and a sleepy-headed Kitty came in. She did not want to talk; she just wanted company. Fabienne extended an arm and the little girl came and climbed on to her lap and snuggled down to finish her sleep out.

Fabienne looked down at the sleeping child and stroked the hair back from her forehead, and tried hard to remind herself that this job was only temporary. It was only June yet, and quite some while to go before the start of the school summer holidays. The holidays would last for about six weeks, but would Rachel be able to cope by herself at the end of that time? Will I, Fabienne began to wonder—her heartstrings pulled so much after less than a week of being at Brackendale—be able to just walk away?

Incredibly, visions of Vere Tolladine sprang into her head. Good grief! It was as if she included him, as if, when the time came for her to leave Brackendale permanently, she would be hard put to it to leave him, too!

Weird, she decided! And was glad when Kitty stirred and got down from her lap to go and get washed and dressed. Fabienne used her hairdrier to finish off drying her hair and, when all she was going to do that morning was to get into her car and drive home to Lintham, it took her some while to decide what to wear.

When she and the twins went down to breakfast, Fabienne was wearing a well-cut pair of stylish white trousers which suited her long legs and neat behind, and was matched with a cropped white jacket which set that behind off to perfection. Her hair she had pulled back from her face, and elegantly arranged to fall long and shining to the middle of her shoulders.

She was uncertain, this not being a work day, that Vere would be down to breakfast at his usual time. But he was there, dark-haired and handsome and, if she wasn't very much mistaken from the look on his face, in brooding mood.

Ridiculously her heart skipped a couple of beats. 'Good morning,' she greeted him pleasantly, and discovered that her impression that he was not full of the joys that morning had been close to accurate.

She saw his unsmiling glance go over her as the children went and settled themselves in their places at the table and guessed that he had taken in her outfit and the fresh look of her when, 'No one would ever know you'd had a disturbed night!' he grunted, obviously not meaning it as a compliment.

What the hell? 'One couldn't say the same about you!' she retorted, and saw that that had gone down about as well as a septic foot. 'Say good morning to your uncle, children,' she instructed them and, while Vere was managing to find something pleasant to say to the children, she took her own place at the table. Recalling the awareness of him she had experienced, she was glad that he would never know just how disturbed last night had truly been.

Breakfast was well under way, with John, Fabienne was pleased to see, seeming to have forgotten all about his nightmare. In fact, and hearteningly he and his twin were indulging in the first healthy squabble she'd heard pass between them, and she took her attention from them and glanced across to Vere.

If she had thought that he would have had his eyes on the children if anywhere, Fabienne discovered that she was very much mistaken. For Vere, his look no less brooding, was looking at no one but her.

He did not speak, and Fabienne discovered that nerves—which she had never suffered from before in her life—were causing her to rush headlong into speech. 'The children,' she said abruptly, and slowed down to ask, 'Who's looking after them this...?' Her words faded at his harsh look.

'That's my concern, not yours,' he replied.

Why she didn't tell him there and then that he could have that concern permanently because she wasn't coming back, she didn't know, because it was hovering there on the tip of her tongue. She opened her mouth, and suddenly knew why—large-eyed and earnest, and promised, John stared at her. She smiled at him, and turned and smiled at her employer. 'I wish you joy,' she said sweetly, and entered a conversation with the children on whether eating one's crust really *did* make one's hair grow curly.

'You've got—nice hair,' John said in that husky voice of his.

'Why, thank you, sweetheart,' she smiled gently, though could not resist taking a peek at Vere to see if he, too, was looking at her hair and might, too, think it was nice. He wasn't even looking. Swine, she dubbed him, and still thought him so when later she went upstairs to pick up her weekend bag.

He was nowhere to be seen when, the twins going with her to wave her off, she went out to her car. She kissed them both, and again endorsed—more for John's sake than for Kitty's—that she'd be there again when they got up on Monday morning.

'See you Monday,' she said again as they stood back and she started up the ignition. She drove away, somehow feeling oddly reluctant. Now wasn't that odd? she mused. Why, when Vere Tolladine was such a positive pig, should she feel strangely pulled to stay?

Fabienne was feeling happier by the time she had pulled her car up on the drive of her own home. What with the dog going into raptures to see her, not to mention the loving welcome she got from her parents, she defied anyone to stay down.

'The phone's never stopped ringing since you went,' her mother informed her during coffee and after an indepth question and answer session.

'Tom Walton rang me at Brackendale.'

'I thought it would be all right to give him your number. Hannah rang. She said can you give her a buzz the moment you get in—something to do with a dress she wants your opinion on.'

'Guess who's going shopping this afternoon,' Fabienne laughed. However, with a glance at the adoring Oliver, 'Though only after I've taken you for a long walk.'

Fabienne, after an afternoon dress-shopping with her friend Hannah, spent the evening playing boule with Hannah and Tom and a few more friends.

The weather took a change for the worse the next day but, with Oliver more keen on looking for imaginary vermin than on whether it rained, she took him for another walk.

To her delight her brother was paying them a visit when she got back. 'How long have you been here?' she asked in pleasure.

'Just arrived. Going to make me a cup of tea?'

Her mother was already getting to her feet but all at once Fabienne sensed that Alex particularly wanted her to be the one to make the tea. 'I'll do it,' she said, and was in the kitchen before her mother could stop her.

Alex joined her there a minute or so later. 'How's the job going?' he enquired.

'You'll never believe it, but I like it.'

'Never quite saw you as a nanny, myself,' he agreed. 'How's the mother's help bit coming along?' he added, almost as an afterthought—and Fabienne looked at him. Despite the ten-year gap in their ages, she was very close to her brother. His question, she felt, was not an idle one.

'How do you mean?' she asked carefully.

'Well—Rachel. She's not well, is she?'

'She's having a tough time of it,' Fabienne admitted. 'Though she did have one good day last week—I'm hoping it will be two next week.'

'You're a good kid,' he commented with brotherly affection—and then their mother came in to tell them that there was a fruit cake in the tin.

It was raining heavily when Fabienne left Lintham around seven. At the start of her journey her thoughts were on her family, and on Alex in particular. She had never heard him express an interest in any female since his divorce, so could not help but feel pleased that it looked as though he might be getting over Victoria. Not that to enquire after Rachel was taking an interest, exactly—yet, since Alex would as often as not make his own cup of tea rather than ask anyone else to do it, it seemed to her that his request stemmed from his wanting a few words of private conversation.

From there Fabienne's thoughts dwelt on Rachel and on how down she was just now. In no time at all, then, thoughts of Vere were in her head. He had been in a swinish mood yesterday morning—it was to be hoped something had cheered him up over the weekend. Her brow wrinkled.

She drove into the village of Sutton Ash somehow not at ease with the thought that perhaps some weekend visitor to Brackendale—some female visitor—had brightened up Vere Tolladine's lot. Nor did she feel any more comfortable with the thought that maybe he'd gone to London and had a wild weekend there.

Drat the man, she fumed as she garaged her car at Brackendale and braved the pouring rain to dash across the yard into the house—as if she cared!

The dull, overcast sky had made the interior of the house dark and, having managed to dodge most of the rainspots, Fabienne went along the minor hall, her weekend bag in one hand, switching lights on and off as she went with the other.

The house was silent, though since the security deadlock had not been activated she guessed that Vere was not yet in. A moment later, however, and Fabienne was re-evaluating that thought and realising that the house had not yet been finally secured for the night because the one person not yet in was her. For as she neared the study, so she could see that the door was open, and that the light was on.

For no reason she could think of, Fabienne had to swallow on a suddenly dry throat before she could go on. And, having gone on, having reached the study, it seemed that her feet simply refused to allow her to go on past until she had looked in.

With quickening heartbeats she saw that Vere was in there. He was seated behind the large desk, not working but, pen in hand, looking straight to the door, his gaze directly on to her.

She told herself it would be churlish to pass by without a word. 'See, I told you I'd come back,' she stated chirpily, and saw that his swinish mood had not lifted any in her absence.

'Not before time, either,' he snarled, his eyes on the slender figure she made in her cream silk shirt and stylish red crêpe skirt, mid-calf-length and slit to the knee.

'Did I miss something?' she stayed to enquire.

'Like two days of rain, plus two cooped-up children in competition to see who could be the most argumentative and bored?' he grunted. That he made no mention of Rachel was indicative that she had kept despondently to her room, Fabienne rather thought. 'How did your weekend go?' he clipped, not seriously interested, she was sure.

'Better than yours by the sound of it,' she murmured drily and—unbelievably—discovered that she must have reached his sense of humour. His mouth picked up at the corners in a half-grin, anyhow.

She felt much cheered, anyway, and would have gone on, only, 'Come in and tell me about it,' he invited, his tone now even, his acid look gone. 'I could do with a break from this,' he added, pointing to the complicated-looking matter spread out on his desk before him.

Her heart softened. To go and chat with him for a minute after the foul couple of days he'd spent with a pair of bored and possibly fractious children was the least she could do.

She dropped her weekend bag down in the hall and entered his study to sit in a chair over by a bookcase filled with business-type books of the sort she hoped she would never have to read.

'There's not a lot to tell.' She smiled, saw his dark glance flick to her mouth and back to her eyes again. 'I went for a walk with Oliver, and shopping with——'

'Oliver?'

'The family hound—well, Jack Russell, actually.'

'You like children *and* animals?'

She grinned. 'Martyr that I am! Though Oliver would be most upset to be called an animal—he regards himself as a very important member of the family. Which,' she added, after a moment's thought, 'is, I suppose, what he is. Did you know that——?' She broke off. 'I'm rattling on,' she apologised.

'I did ask,' he reminded her. 'So you took your dog for a walk, went shopping, then what?'

'Not a lot, really,' she answered, realising that she was in danger of boring him to tears.

But it seemed that he was really interested. For, 'I thought you said you had a date?' he reminded her. 'Your boyfriend rang here,' he hinted.

'Oh, Tom... Hmm—he's not really a boyfriend. A group of us played boule—Tom rang to remind me.'

'You'd have forgotten?'

She grinned, realised that she had never felt happier. 'Hannah, my friend Hannah, would have given me a reminder when we went shopping yesterday,' she informed him. 'We usually go around in a group.'

'Safety in numbers?' he queried, that rise of his right eyebrow she was growing familiar with appearing once more.

'I'm a big girl now,' she laughed, decrying any suggestion of his idea.

'I——' he began and then, his look most decidedly cool, 'Are you saying that you have frequent affairs?' he demanded.

Her jaw dropped. Never had she ever known anyone so forthright. 'No, I'm not!' she retorted, offended—not that it was any of his business if she did! 'You make me sound like a tart!' she exploded as his question sank deeper in. 'Well, for——'

'Don't be ridiculous!' he rapped. 'I——'

'Oh, go to hell!' she flew, and was furiously on her feet at the same instant that he, too, angrily left his chair.

'Might I remind you that I'm your employer?' he rapped.

'So fire me!' she erupted and as he glared at her, so she glared at him for one furious, highly combustible second before, abruptly, she turned her back on him and went storming to the door. She didn't need this job! He could jolly well stick his job! He——

Having stormed to the door, she knew that to the left lay the outer doors, her car and a loving home. To the right lay the stairs, and her job. Enraged, she went to the right. Not for him, she fumed as she marched up the stairs, but for those children and their mother.

Pig! Swine! She hoped he rotted in hell. She had felt so happy. He had spoilt all that! That he had been furious, too, that she wasn't some meek and mild member of his payroll gave her some satisfaction. Though as she went along the landing to her bedroom and looked over the elegant handrail to the floor below she saw that Vere was standing in his study doorway watching her—and any scrap of satisfaction she experienced went flying. Because as she stared mutinously at him, so she was certain that, while he tried his level best to keep his expression serious, the humour of the situation was getting to him. At any rate, just before he abruptly turned to go back into his study, she would swear that his face broke up.

The swine, the diabolical swine! He was not furious—he was laughing at her!

Fabienne came the closest she had ever come just then to giving up her job. But something, and she was not into deciding what just then, kept her there. Her glance then went to the doors of the children's rooms and her anger against Vere suddenly evaporated. The door to John's room had been left ajar. Vere, she instinctively knew, had left that door open for John's feeling of security and also so that he should hear him if the child cried out.

By the time she got into bed a couple of hours later, Fabienne had been over again every word that had passed between her and Vere that evening, and she was again angry. She punched her pillow, wishing it were his head. Perhaps she might have acted differently if she had been in an 'employed' situation before, or if she had truly financially needed this job—though she rather doubted it. The nerve of him, to suggest that she had lovers by the dozen! Who the devil did he think he was?

She was about to put out her light when she suddenly began to wonder just what she was so upset about, and again she dissected their conversation. 'Oh, grief,' she muttered five minutes later. No way had he implied that she was a tart!

Fabienne put out her light and lay down and was swamped by confusion. What the dickens was it about the man that, when she had always been for the most part even-tempered, he barely had to say a couple of words out of place and she was up in arms? What was it about the man that in split-seconds he could have her all emotional over nothing? What was it about him that the man could so swiftly, so effortlessly, shatter her equilibrium? She had not come up with any answer when she fell asleep.

As if by magic, after so much rain, it was a beautiful sunny morning when Fabienne opened her eyes. 'You came back!' exclaimed a happy, husky voice, and she sat up in bed to see that John, wearing the first truly happy smile she had seen on him, was standing at the bottom of her bed.

'Didn't I say I would?' she smiled back, and the day got off to a good start.

She was, however, slightly ashamed of what she now saw as her unprovoked eruption of the evening before as she and the twins later entered the breakfast-room. 'Good morning,' she greeted Vere crisply as they took their seats.

He favoured her with a baleful look. 'Trust the sun to be shining,' he grunted.

'It always does on the righteous,' she replied sweetly, in no doubt that he was referring to the wet weekend with two fretful children.

'Give it time,' he gritted, and got up from his chair, ruffled two shiny heads in passing and, as Fabienne burst out laughing, went off to work.

With the day starting off so well from the way she was looking at it, things were much improved, she decided, as it began to dawn on her that she found her exchanges with Vere quite stimulating.

The day went even better, in that when she returned from taking the children to school—having declined Lyndon Davies' offer of lunch, this time—she found that Rachel was up and dressed and doing her utmost to be positive.

'I really meant to be up in time to go with you to school,' she apologised, 'but those wretched tablets make it difficult for me to get going straight away.'

'Don't worry about it,' Fabienne smiled. 'Perhaps tomorrow.'

'Perhaps,' Rachel agreed. 'I *am* making progress, honestly I am, but it's a sort of two steps forward, one step back kind of progress. Though I'm heaps better than the mess I was at Easter when Vere...' Her voice tailed of. 'Come on, let's go for a walk or something,' she suggested.

'Yes, let's,' Fabienne encouraged, delighted at the positive effort Rachel was making.

It was gradually, during their walk, that Fabienne learned that Rachel originally came from a village not more than a half hour's car journey from Lintham.

'Are your parents still there?' she queried tentatively, not wanting to upset her if they were dead.

'We—don't get on,' Rachel replied haltingly.

'Oh, I'm sorry,' Fabienne murmured sympathetically.

Rachel sighed. 'In a way, so am I now. I've thought lately that I really should make an effort and get in touch with them again.'

'Perhaps I could drive you over to see them one day,' Fabienne suggested, trying to be helpful. Rachel had her own car, which Vere had had brought to Brackendale for her, but she did not feel up to driving just yet. 'I could leave you and go and see my mother for an hour and pick you up on the way back,' she warmed to her theme.

'I...' Rachel hesitated. Then, 'I'm—not ready yet.'

'No hurry,' Fabienne stated easily.

'We had a row,' Rachel went on. 'They were right, of course, and I knew that they were right, but...' Her voice started to falter, and while Fabienne was so very tempted to suggest that she leave it there and say no more, she somehow sensed it would be more helpful for Rachel to start to talk whatever it was out of her system. Rachel took a steadying breath, and then blurted out bluntly, 'Nick, my husband, was a womaniser—first-class. I knew it, of course, but didn't thank my father for having a go at Nick for not treating me better.'

'You quarrelled,' Fabienne put in quietly.

'I flew off the handle and, regardless of all the love they had always showed me, I told both my parents to keep out of my business.'

'They didn't come to Nick's funeral?'

She shook her head. 'They know me well. I didn't want them there.'

'Things will get better one day,' Fabienne promised, and received a faint smile for her efforts.

'Shall we go back to the house?' Rachel suggested, and Fabienne knew that Rachel had had enough for one day.

It did not surprise her that she kept to her room when the time came for her to collect the children from school. It did surprise her, though, that as she sat outside on a garden bench and watched while some yards away the twins played on the lawn in the sun, Rachel should come out to join her and, for the first time, looking all sparkly-eyed—shiny eyes that had nothing to do with unshed tears.

Fabienne was just thinking how their walk that morning must have done more good for her than she had thought when Rachel remembered, 'Oh, by the way, Alex phoned while you were out.'

'Did he?' Fabienne enquired, pleased he had rung but sorry that she had missed him. 'Did he ring for anything special?'

'To remind you that it's your father's sixtieth birthday in two weeks' time.'

How odd! She wouldn't dream of forgetting her father's birthday. It was a week on Sunday, and they'd planned a big family lunch with aunts and uncles and some friends of both her father and mother. 'That's typical Alex,' she reflected. 'He's so thoughtful. Not that I would have forgotten.'

Rachel was looking across to the twins. 'He's divorced, isn't he?' she questioned absently.

Fabienne hesitated. Alex was special. But she guessed he must have told Rachel that himself and anyhow, loyalty apart, Rachel had opened up to her that day and friendship was a two-way street. 'Yes, he is,' she replied and, whether Rachel was truly interested or not, 'He has a son, Philip, a year older than Kitty and John, but he's having a few "rights of access" problems.'

'Oh, how awful. I didn't know...'

'Alex will sort it out, I expect, but it's such a shame, and so unnecessary. I've always liked Victoria, his wife— ex-wife, I should say—but——' Fabienne dried up, her loyalty to her brother such that she thought she had said enough. She looked over to where Kitty and John had tired of their game and were starting to irritate each other. 'How long is it since you've played rounders?' she asked Rachel.

'Four of us?'

Fabienne looked over to where the gardener was busy at work. 'Bob looks the fit type,' she remarked of the fifty-year-old man, 'I'd bet he'd much rather play ball than hoe that lupin bed.'

'You wouldn't!'

For a bonus Rachel joined them for dinner that evening, too. Fabienne couldn't be off noticing how courteously and gently Vere behaved towards Rachel, and for a few moments fell into a most peculiar reverie where she wanted Vere to be gentle to her, too, instead of the brutish swine he so easily turned into whenever they had any dealings on a one-to-one basis.

'And Fenne——' She jerked out of her peculiar thoughts on hearing John speaking her name.

'Fenne?' his uncle queried.

'Fabienne says it's all right to call her that if we want to,' John explained with an anxious look, as if he had been impolite.

'Fabienne's a bit of a mouthful sometimes for a seven-year-old,' Fabienne burst in protectively.

Vere gave her a quirky look, as though to say, put your ruffled feathers down, and thereafter proceeded to ignore her as he asked his nephew, 'So what did Fenne do?'

'Fenne said we were going to play rounders, and we did,' Kitty took up. 'And Bob was just, just brilliant and in my team, and he scored six, and——'

'Bob?' Vere asked faintly. But while Fabienne realised that confession-time was at hand, she discovered her confession was not necessary, because, fast as ever with his deductions, Vere scored a direct hit when, with a cool glance over in her direction he guessed, 'I'll bet it was Fenne who said he'd be a jolly good fielder.'

'She did!' John agreed eagerly. 'Bob seemed a bit—a bit shy at first, but Fenne told him that he could hoe his old lupin bed any old time and——'

Fabienne felt it was time that she spoke up. 'Bob was most reluctant to leave his duties,' she stated clearly. And, as Vere's cool grey eyes pinned her with a steady look, she tilted her chin and added, 'I accept full responsibility.'

For a couple of long, tense seconds she held eye-contact with him, half expecting to be dismissed on the spot for taking his staff away from the work they were engaged to do, but—and she had to own it was a relief—'Who else?' was all he said.

Fabienne went to her bed that night wondering about that 'Who else?'. She rather felt that in those two simple words she had been told off. As if, feeling unable to go for her jugular in front of two children who were starting to recover from trauma, he was saying 'who else' but her would have such almighty cheek!

Her good intentions to give Bob a hand with his weeding the next day proved a non-starter when the day dawned grey, gloomy and decidedly wet. Rachel, however, maintained her good spirits of the previous day, though when the children came home from school and started bickering she sent Fabienne a pleading look and left her to cope.

Fabienne was discovering that John, although for the most part malleable, had a stubborn streak that was rock-solid. Kitty would push him, but only so far, and then he would round on her. The next day was as dreadful weatherwise as the day before and Fabienne had left the twins watching TV in the next-door room, while she tidied up the after-school chaos in Kitty's room, when all hell broke loose.

In a flash she was in the playroom. 'She started it!' John got in first, that look about him that said it would be best to wait a while before delving into the crime.

What could she do? For a start, Fabienne decided, throw away all the textbooks on how to deal with temper tantrums, and try a bit of good old-fashioned bribery.

'So—who's coming down to the village with me for an ice-cream?' she asked, and crossed her fingers that neither of them would remember that Mrs Hobbs probably had a freezer compartment full of ice-cream.

But, '*Me*!' Kitty yelled at once.

'I'm not taking the car,' Fabienne warned, knowing that they would have been to the village and back and could be back to square one inside twenty minutes if she did that.

'We're walking—in the rain?' John queried, losing some of his mulish look and starting to look interested.

'We'll have to wear our wellies and raincoats,' she answered.

An hour later she and two laughing and animated children were walking back up the drive. There and back they had walked the best part of two miles, demolished ice-creams in no time, splashed in puddles, were drenched—and happy.

She was happy herself, Fabienne realised—and just then noticed that Vere's car was standing on the drive. He was home early. The happiness in her took on a warmer glow.

'We'd better go in the back way,' she instructed the twins. 'We can leave our wellingtons in the rear hall for now.'

Feeling strangely comforted to know that Vere was home, Fabienne opened the rear door supposing that, whether home early or late, she would not see him until dinner-time. And then stopped dead.

'Hello, trouble!' Vere greeted them, and as they trooped in she realised that he must have been in the kitchen having some conversation with Mrs Hobbs.

'Hello, Uncle Vere!' the twins chorused and, while he attended to divesting John of his rainwear and Fabienne assisted Kitty, they excitedly told him of their ice-cream adventure.

'Pop into the kitchen and get Mrs Hobbs to dry your faces and anything else that needs a towelling,' he instructed them indulgently—and as they went off to see another of their favourite people he turned his attention to Fabienne. 'Just look at you!' he commented, looking down into her damp, upturned face.

'They say rainwater's good for the complexion,' she laughed, uncaring that she had not a scrap of make-up on.

His eyes roved her face, her skin, her features, and then he made her heart race by solemnly declaring, 'Yours doesn't need any help.'

She wanted to swallow, but couldn't. Felt transfixed, couldn't move, couldn't speak, yet knew she had to say something—and chose to tell him the only thing to come into her head—even though the children had already told him. 'We've been to the village for ice-creams.'

'In this weather?' he questioned, and to her delight there was a definite gleam of amusement in his look.

'Why not?' she tossed back at him with a grin.

'You didn't think that perhaps Mrs Hobbs' freezer could have saved you the journey?'

'If you don't tell the children, I won't,' she laughed, and was riveted when the most wonderful smile broke on his face.

Impulsively then, or so it seemed, his head came down and, causing her heart to thunder, he placed a light kiss on her gently parted lips. 'You're a child yourself,' he told her—and she wasn't having that.

Without thinking she stretched up and placed her mouth warmly against his. She felt his hands come to

her waist, grip and hold, felt his mouth move against
hers and was just about to hold on to him when
somehow, perhaps by mutual consent, they broke apart.

Her head was anywhere; yet again she knew she should
say something. By happy chance, from somewhere she
found an impish grin and, aware that there had been
nothing childlike in her kiss to him, 'Say that again!'
she teased.

Vere's glance went from her eyes down to her inviting
mouth and, 'Be off with you, woman,' he growled. 'You
could harm a man's sanity.'

Fabienne's head was in a whirl as she dressed to go
down to dinner that night. She could still feel Vere's lips
against her own, still feel a tingle from that touch. Oh,
lord, what was happening to her?

For the first time she regretted that she had only a
limited wardrobe with her at Brackendale. But, dressed
with the greatest of care, she went down to dinner with
Rachel and the children—only to discover that Vere was
not there, that he had gone out.

Disappointment hit her like a body-blow as she recalled that while he usually garaged his car round at the
rear of the house it had been standing on the front drive
when she and the twins had come in. Obviously he'd
come home early because he'd got some heavy date lined
up.

A *frisson* of anger stirred in her, and Fabienne realised
that she did not at all like the idea of him with some
other woman. A moment later, however, and she was
aghast at herself. Good grief, it was nothing to do with
her—she was just the hired help, and no more than that.
And, heaven save us, that was all she wanted to be! Most
definitely!

CHAPTER FIVE

FOR some totally unknown reason Fabienne discovered she was experiencing a most unexpected shyness when, with the twins in tow, she went down to breakfast the following morning.

Vere was there, but although his greeting to Kitty and John was affable she detected a glint of cold steel in the look he flicked her way. His answer to her quiet 'Good morning' was little more than a grunt.

Be like that, she fumed, and could not have been better pleased that, by the look of it, his date of the previous evening seemed to have soured him.

It was not, however, his date that was at fault, she discovered that evening, but herself! He was quite friendly with everyone else, conversing amicably with the children and Rachel at dinner—but not with her.

Fabienne felt more than a little shaken by this turn of events, and told herself that she was being over-sensitive, imagining it. But, as she 'watched points' at breakfast on Friday and at dinner in the evening, too, there was no mistaking in her mind that, while Vere observed every courtesy and politeness with her in front of the others so that she was certain that they would have no idea that she was being cold-shouldered, *she* knew.

'I think I'll go home tonight, if no one minds,' she said out of the blue just as everyone was finishing the pudding course. She skimmed a glance at Vere from beneath her long lashes, and found the idea of driving up to Lintham setting like concrete. His glance back at her was cool, dispassionate, and Fabienne knew that any chance he might again ask, 'You *do* intend to come back?' was laughable. She slid her eyes from him—no one was going to see her hurt, least of all him—and her gaze lit on the twins. John was looking anxious again, she saw, so she smiled and assured him, 'I'll see you two reprobates first thing on Monday morning.'

Immediately he looked relieved. 'What's a repr——?'

Fabienne phoned her parents to tell them that she'd see them in a couple of hours, and drove to Lintham almost praying that they would have a continual monsoon in Sutton Ash that weekend and that the twins, who were now growing daily more lively and more like any other seven-year-olds, would drive one Vere Tolladine up the wall.

To her chagrin, summer returned the next day. She doubted, since Sutton Ash was not all that far away, that her monsoon hopes would be fulfilled. She spent the rest of the day wishing that she could think about something other than that wretched man and his cold attitude towards her.

'Anything wrong, love?' her mother asked as they loaded the dishwasher Sunday morning.

'Wrong?'

'You seem a bit preoccupied.'

'Really?' Her mother was just one wonderful person and Fabienne had always felt able to confide absolutely anything in her. But, 'Nothing wrong,' she smiled, somehow unable this time to share her most intimate worries. 'Other than, of course——' just in case her mother would not swallow that '—I'm constantly trying to think up new games to keep Kitty and John amused.'

That was true. But it was odd, Fabienne thought as she took Oliver for a walk, that even though Vere was being such a brute to her she should feel she would not mind at all getting back early.

She did not do so, however. Oliver saw to that. Because of his proclivity to visit his ladyfriends or to take himself off ratting when the mood was on him, the hedges in the garden had been wired, netted, and wired again. But he was a born escaper and, sensing he was being ignored when Fabienne's aunt and uncle paid them a visit, he tunnelled out and was discovered missing late that afternoon.

'I'll go,' Fabienne volunteered, knowing her errand to find him could take hours, just as she knew that, left to his own devices, he would come home when he was good and ready. But that wasn't the point; Oliver was family.

It was eight o'clock before she found him—as happy as Larry and wagging his tail—and half-past eight before she was ready to head back to Sutton Ash. 'Do you think you should ring to tell them what time to expect you?' her mother asked.

'I've got a key, so it won't matter if I'm late back,' she assured them.

Not much, she discovered, when she inserted her key in the rear door of Brackendale—and found that it would not open! For all that the outside light was on, the security lock was on. The door had been locked for the night—and she knew who had done it!

Nothing like being made welcome, she fumed, and that was when all her pent-up feelings at the stiff and starchy, not to say hostile way Vere Tolladine was behaving reared up.

It was touch and go, then, that she did not go back to her car and head straight back to Lintham. But there was her promise to John she'd see him first thing on Monday morning and—dammit—who did Vere Tolladine think he was, kissing her one minute and acting so downright anti the next?

She stabbed a finger at the doorbell and pressed hard. Out of consideration for anyone who might be asleep, though, she felt obliged to take her finger off the bell after a second or two. She waited.

She did not have to wait long, but her anger was in no way tempered when she heard the locking mechanism being released and then the door being opened.

As she had suspected, Vere was still up and stood, chisel-featured, looking down at her. 'You did expect me to come back?' she charged shortly.

'At a reasonable hour,' he grated and impatiently stood aside for her to enter.

Ye gods, Fabienne fumed as she crossed the threshold, some nights *he* did not come home until gone midnight! He was not, it seemed, of a mind to hang about to listen to any more of her sharp remarks, but secured the doors and, without a word of goodnight, went striding off up the hall, leaving her to take herself off to her bed.

Ignorant swine, she chafed hotly and, having exchanged her weekend bag for a slightly larger case, case in hand, she went smartly after him.

He was in his study, the other side of his desk and about to sit down when she went, without apology, straight in. Vere did not take his seat, however, nor did he this time wish her to be seated; she could tell that from the direct antagonistic look he threw her.

'Well?' he rapped, and she wanted to hit him.

She took a controlling breath. 'I am not,' she said distinctly, 'a tart.'

His direct dark gaze seemed to her to become even more piercing. 'We've had this conversation before!' he clipped, unmistakably a man who wanted to get on with some work and had no time or inclination to go in for repeat conversations.

Well, tough! 'Pardon me for being boring!' she flew. 'But last Wednesday you kissed me and ever since then——'

'Last Wednesday I kissed you,' he agreed sharply, 'a peck, no more—and you, you came on to me in——' He broke off, those all-seeing dark eyes fixed nowhere but on her face. 'How odd you should blush,' he resumed, 'when——'

'Damn you!' Fabienne flared, aware that her face was scarlet. But whose face wouldn't be, to be so accused? 'I've never "come on", as you call it, to any man in my life!'

'You wouldn't call that kiss *you* gave me a——' he began to retort sceptically, but halted, and was still as he considered what she had just said. But, as ever, it did not take him long to weigh up the pros and cons, and scepticism was back with a vengeance when, 'You're a virgin?' he scoffed.

Why the blazes she was suddenly afflicted with a massive propensity to blush defeated her as colour flared in her cheeks again. Although it was true he was the only man she knew who could make her so emotionally out of balance that any chance remark he made could trigger it.

She picked up her suitcase, unaware that she had dropped it down, and with a lofty, 'Some of us are!' she did not deign to stay and argue with him, but turned about and went up to her room.

Fabienne lay awake for a long time that night. She could not be sorry that she had let go with some of the anger that had been building up in her, but it had solved nothing. She had worked out for herself that Vere's hostile attitude had only come about since that kiss, and he, tonight, had just confirmed it.

All too obviously he was regretting that 'peck' that
had triggered her 'coming on' to him, cheeky swine, and
was at pains to show her that all he wanted from her
was a business relationship. He should be so lucky to
think that she might want more! Pig!

She was still awake an hour later, but by then some
of her anger had mellowed and, having again been over
everything that had been said, she supposed it wasn't
every employee that told him 'Damn you' and remained
on his payroll.

Fabienne drifted off to sleep feeling no more
comfortable to be living in a house where someone
treated her so coolly, but if—despite this being his home
and not his workplace—he wanted to be totally
businesslike, then so be it. And who cared, anyhow? The
wretched job was only temporary anyway.

John came in to check that she was back early on
Monday morning, and they shared a quick hug which
she reckoned did her as much good as it did him—it was
nice to know that somebody cared—and then it was
action stations as the day got under way.

'Good morning,' she greeted Vere without actually
looking at him as she entered the breakfast-room, and
thereafter ignored him. Well, not quite ignored, she
amended, for the wretched man, she discovered, was
impossible to ignore. But she was careful to keep her
manner, if polite, otherwise aloof.

Not that he seemed to notice, she thought crossly
when, having exchanged barely a word with her, he
passed a few comments with the twins, made a few
pleasant remarks to them in parting, and left for his
office.

Fabienne was feeling decidedly out of sorts as she saw
the children into the school playground. So much so that
she seriously considered accepting Lyndon Davies' in-

vitation to join him in a wine-bar in Haychester that evening.

But, 'Sorry, Lyndon,' she smiled; to drown her sorrows was not her style.

Besides which, what sorrows had she got, for goodness' sake? she wondered as she drove back to Brackendale. Compared to Rachel, her life was a doddle.

Rachel, though, Fabienne discovered when she came out to her as she halted her car, seemed to have made more strides in getting better. 'Glad to see you back!' she smiled. 'And sorry I couldn't manage to get my head off the pillow to join you for breakfast.'

'Don't worry about it,' Fabienne returned lightly. 'Fancy a run?'

'Why not?'

Rachel really was trying to be very positive, Fabienne saw, and half an hour later they were on their way to Haychester, Rachel of the opinion that she must do something to steer her daughter's tastes away from shocking-pink socks.

In view of the fact that all Rachel's days might still be merging into one Fabienne tactfully held back on asking what sort of a weekend she'd had. When Rachel asked, she talked freely of her own weekend, though.

'Your family sound nice,' Rachel volunteered when she had finished telling her of her aunt and uncle's visit, and Oliver's escape in pique.

'They are—I'm lucky.' Fabienne smiled.

'They're lucky, too,' Rachel stated, and Fabienne thought that that was very nice of her. 'Er—did you see anything of your brother over the weekend?'

Fabienne shook her head. 'He had Philip for the weekend and they went off to do manly things together.'

With Rachel saying that she was pleased about that they shopped for a few items of clothing for the twins, stopped for coffee, and then took advantage of the beautiful gardens near to the centre of Haychester, and of some summer sun.

There were other like-minded people about, but no one sitting close by when Rachel suddenly said, 'I suppose what I should really be doing instead of sitting here is to go on to my own house and open it up to give it an airing.'

This was positive stuff, indeed, but Fabienne, who knew so very little about depression, was overwhelmingly aware that she must tread very carefully. 'I'll—er—come with you any time if you like,' she offered quietly.

'Not yet!' Rachel immediately backed away from the idea.

'No hurry,' Fabienne replied easily.

And all was quiet between them for about a minute and then Rachel, in a terse, quiet voice, was all at once blurting out, 'He promised me he would never look at another woman!' Fabienne quickly cottoned on that Rachel was talking about her dead husband, and Rachel, still in that same tense voice, hurried on, 'He vowed he loved only me. Swore that he was broken-hearted to have hurt me, and how he would never, ever hurt me again—and I, I like the trusting idiot I was, believed him.'

'Perhaps—perhaps he was being sincere,' Fabienne ventured gently.

'How sincere was he that, while swearing he would never be unfaithful again, he should have his mistress of the moment in the car with him when he died?' Rachel asked.

'Rachel—I'm so sorry,' Fabienne whispered.

'There's more, but I won't sully your ears with it.' Rachel stared into the distance, without really seeing, Fabienne felt sure and, tonelessly now, she went on.

'Over the first few weeks—after he died—I found out more and more about my "loving" husband. When I learned, though, that he'd actually taken one of his women to our marriage bed while we, the children and I, were away for a few days, it all seemed too much.'

Fabienne felt at a loss to know what to say that might be helpful. Perhaps, though, it might be cathartic, now that Rachel had started to talk of what must have been bottled up inside her, to encourage her a little more. Even as she prompted, 'So you decided to stay with your step-brother-in-law for a little while?' she confessed that she felt most uncertain.

'It wasn't quite like that. By the time I, with Kitty and John, moved into Brackendale, I wasn't up to making any sort of clear-cut decision. Vere had been in regular contact since Nick died, checking to see that we wanted for nothing and generally keeping an eye on us he's been so good to us, you wouldn't believe. Anyhow, he asked what we were doing for Christmas and I was feeling so mentally bruised and battered by then that I wanted nothing to do with anyone connected with Nick Hargreaves, so I lied and said I was spending Christmas with my parents.'

'Only you haven't—um—made your peace with them yet.'

'True. God, why are parents always right?'

'They've lived longer,' Fabienne suggested, and was rewarded with a faint smile, then Rachel took a shaky breath, and continued.

'So we managed to get through Christmas and put up a good front when in the new year Vere rang or—less frequently—called to see us. I truly felt then that things must improve as time went by.'

'But they didn't?'

Rachel shook her head. 'I still didn't want to admit that I couldn't cope when for a lot of February and March Vere had to be abroad on business. So we didn't see him until Easter when he called with Easter eggs—he must have been absolutely appalled at the neglected state of the house, not to mention the neglected state of the twins.'

'He asked you to come to Brackendale?' Fabienne suggested.

'He didn't stop to ask—by then I wasn't up to making even the smallest decision. In fact, looking back, I can barely remember anything of his visit save that he was there and next *we* weren't, and that all in the same instant, or so it seems now, he had medical people coming to Brackendale and checking us—me and the children—over. He—Vere—enrolled the children at the village school, employed extra domestic help and was generally marvellous. As, too, was Mrs Hobbs. Anyway, we limped along until half-term—not that my contribution was anything at all—and that was where you came in.'

'Me? The children weren't on half——'

'They were away from school at half-term, wandering around like lost souls, when Vere realised that since I wasn't up to coping yet it might be an idea to engage someone to keep an eye on Kitty and John during the coming school holiday. And——' Rachel smiled '—I'm glad he chose you.'

Fabienne smiled back and then a young couple came and sat nearby, within hearing distance, and she knew that Rachel's confidences were at an end.

It *had* seemed to have done Rachel some good, though, Fabienne felt, when at dinner Rachel kept up her 'two paces forward' recovery and was quite talkative for her. Kitty and John were chatty too, she noted. Which, since Vere was saying little—to her at any rate—and since she had nothing she wanted to say to him either, made it just as well that somebody had something to say.

At one juncture, however, she somehow felt that his eyes were on her. But when she flicked a glance his way, his head turned towards Kitty and he was listening to her holding forth on something that had happened at school that day.

Bizarrely, Fabienne felt her heartbeats flutter as she looked at his strong, aristocratic face. She liked him, even while she oft-times hated him. In all honesty she knew that she liked him—so why couldn't he like her?

Unconsciously she sighed—and cursed the sound, for he, his hearing more acute than she would have believed, heard it and at once turned his head to look at her. My God, add 'arrogant' to that 'aristocratic', she thought and, as she stared back, refusing to look away, she tilted her head an arrogant fraction, too.

'Do you have a problem?' he enquired courteously.

Nothing a twelve-bore shotgun would not put right, she thought sourly, not thanking him that, because there were other people present, he was keeping his hostility in check.

'Not a thing,' she replied sweetly, and saw his glance flick to her smiling mouth, but knew he had belief in neither her smile nor her sweet reply.

Rachel had a down day the next day but Fabienne thought, on going to see her, that somehow her down days did not seem to be so deep-down as they had just two weeks ago.

She declined to go with Fabienne to pick up the children from school that afternoon, though, and as it was such a beautiful day Fabienne decided to walk rather than use the car. And, because the children had a mile to walk back, too, she treated them to ice-creams and absolved her conscience by deciding that they were overdue for a little spoiling.

Their chatter on the way home was full of excitement because they had both been invited to Sadie Bragg's birthday party tomorrow afternoon. 'She wasn't going to have one,' Kitty confided, 'but her mother said she could last night, so we're all going.'

'That will be nice,' Fabienne murmured, and as they walked through the drive gates at Brackendale so she recognised her brother's car coming away from the house. 'Alex—I missed you!' she exclaimed in regret as he stopped his car and got out to say hello and farewell to all three of them.

'Not to worry, Rachel gave me the cup of tea I was gasping for. Everything all right?'

'Fine.'

'Good. See you.' With a hug and a kiss he was back in his car.

Fabienne stood at the gates waving to him as the twins, seeing their mother on the drive coming towards them, ran to meet her to tell her about the party invitation, and then ran off to tell Mrs Hobbs.

'Sorry you missed Alex. If you'd gone in the car...' She smiled and left the rest unsaid and Fabienne, delighted to see that Rachel appeared much more cheered than she had first thing, smiled back.

'Not to worry—I reckon he only called in for a piece of Mrs Hobbs' cake.'

Fabienne dressed with care for dinner that night—and just could not understand the feeling of deflation she felt that Vere was not in to dinner that evening. Good heavens, it was as though she actually *enjoyed* having the hostile brute look down his arrogant nose at her!

She saw him the following morning, though, and *hostile* just wasn't the word for it! For the first time in the two and a half weeks she'd been there she overslept, and could not seem to make up the lost time.

'You two go down to breakfast,' she instructed Kitty and John and, intending to skip her own breakfast so as to be able to deliver them to school on time, 'I'll be down soon.' She knew that Mrs Hobbs would see to them if she was not there but, in any case, there was always their uncle.

And a not very sunny-humoured uncle, she saw, when she later hastened down the stairs to where, having delayed his own start, he was ushering the children out of the house and to where his car was standing.

'I'll take them to school!' she protested, and would have followed after them but, his brow as black as thunder, Vere halted slap-bang in front of her. 'There's no need for you to take them,' she dug her toes in, refusing to feel intimidated by his murderous expression. 'Grief—I only overslept and——'

'And invited one of your men-friends to this house!' he chopped her off unceremoniously.

'What...?' she gasped faintly, and only then started to become aware that Vere's furious mood might have nothing to do with the fact that she had overslept.

'Is it your habit to invite your male friends here so you can kiss and cuddle on my doorstep?' he demanded.

'I——' she began, only broke off as it just then dawned on her that Kitty and John must have told him of Alex's visit yesterday. She had thought that they had understood that he was her brother. But, in the rush of seeing Alex and of him being on his way again, clearly not. 'That——' she began again, but Vere was plainly more incensed the more he thought about it, and again he unceremoniously chopped her off.

'Did you kiss this man?' he demanded. 'Did you have your arms around each other?'

Fabienne most definitely did not like his tone, nor the aggression that went with it. She was not used to it and, what was more, as her aggression rose up to meet his, she was not going to take it!

'What of it?' she challenged, her chin tilted defiantly, sparks of anger flashing in her eyes.

But his eyes were ablaze with a furnace of fury when, going straight for her jugular, 'Might I remind you,' he grated, 'that you're employed here to look after the twins' welfare!'

'I jolly well——' she tried to get in—only he would not let her.

'And that,' he clipped, 'includes their moral welfare!'

He was suggesting that she was immoral! 'How dare you?' she shrieked.

'I dare,' he roared, 'because I will not have you embracing your lovers, and God knows who else, in front of those two innocent children!'

'Then you can go to hell!' she yelled straight back. 'I'm entitled to some free time—and, for that matter, callers!'

His eyes narrowed, and she waited for him to tell her to pack. But, when she was sure it was in his mind to tell her to be out of her room and out of his house before he returned that night, he took one long and controlling breath, and when he spoke again it was to tell her in clipped fashion, 'I'd be obliged, Miss Preston, if you'd introduce your *callers* to me first.'

He might have control of his fury, but her tongue was still on the loose. 'To see if they're suited to walk these hallowed halls?' she flared.

He did not like that, she could tell by the look of dislike he tossed her way. 'Keep that up, and you won't be walking them yourself for much longer!' he threatened, and turned abruptly about to go striding out to his car.

Fabienne watched him go, and damned him to hell. She might once have told him, 'So fire me,' but she knew precisely then that she just did not want to leave. While he, the moment it suited his book to do so, would throw her out on her ear.

Damn him, she thought again mutinously and, even as she admitted feeling very close to tears, she'd be hanged if she would ever tell him that her 'caller' was her brother.

CHAPTER SIX

DAMN him, Fabienne fumed over the next couple of hours. Just because she and Alex had kissed cheeks in front of Kitty and John, she had had to put up with that! Moral welfare! The sauce of it!

The phone rang; she picked it up. 'Is Rachel there?' grated the man she most liked to hate.

'No, she's not!' Fabienne retorted bluntly—and slammed down the phone.

Two minutes later the humour of the situation struck her. Had she really slammed the phone down on the great Vere Tolladine? A weak laugh escaped her—that really *was* a hanging offence!

Perhaps, as a servant, she had been meant to go and look for Rachel? Mutiny was about her again, but she was spared having to make a decision about whether or not to go looking for Rachel when Rachel came looking for her.

'Vere rang, asking for you,' she informed her.

'I'll ring him back,' Rachel answered, and tentatively suggested, 'Fancy risking your neck with me at the steering-wheel? I need to go into Haychester for gifts for the children to take to this bun-fight this afternoon.'

Half an hour later and Fabienne, delighted at the progress Rachel was making, was seated in the passenger seat of Rachel's car as they set out for Haychester.

Nor did her progress end there for, when on other days a few hours of leaving her depression behind was as much as she could manage, Rachel stayed positive that day for far longer. Rachel it was who drove down to the school to collect the children, and Rachel it was who helped Fabienne wash and change them into 'party clothes', and Rachel it was—admittedly requesting that Fabienne sit in the car with her, too—who drove them down to the village to the party.

'Come in and join the madhouse,' Lyndon Davies urged Fabienne while Rachel asked his sister what time they should pick the children up.

'I think, if you don't mind, I'll decline that one,' she laughed.

'Yet another of my invitations consigned to the scrap-heap!' he sighed. 'I shall not be deterred,' he brightened to tell her. 'I shall keep on trying.'

'Do that,' she answered automatically. 'That was a mistake,' she commented to Rachel as they returned to her car.

'Was that the man who asked you for a date when you first took the children to school?' Rachel asked quietly—and, at the sudden dull change in her tone, Fabienne knew that Rachel had gone back to remember her own, now dead, fast-worker husband.

'I...' Fabienne began helplessly.

'You drive,' Rachel said, and handed her the keys to her car.

All the way back to the house Fabienne racked her brains to try and make Rachel feel better, but nothing she could think to say could minimise the strength of hurt that Rachel was feeling.

'Rachel, I...' She tried anyway when she halted the car at Brackendale.

'I'm all right, Fabienne, don't worry,' Rachel quickly told her. 'In fact, I've—— Seeing that man today, re-cognising him for a similar type to Nick—though perhaps a lot more sincere—well, it's just sort of shaken me to realise what an idiot I was to fall for that sort of a man in the first place. I must have been *blind*!' she ended in hushed tones.

'Oh, Rachel,' Fabienne commiserated gently.

She was not surprised that Rachel went up to her room and stayed there. She would not, Fabienne was fairly certain, be down to dinner that night.

Which, as the next few hours went by, gave her something else to worry about. Neither Kitty nor John were greedy children which, if the parties she'd attended when she'd been a child were anything to go by—and they could not have changed all that much—meant that both of them would be so full up with 'goodies' that they would not want any dinner. And, what was more, it would be plain cruel to insist they come down to the dinner table that night and sit there while she and—it had to be faced—Vere chewed their way through the evening meal.

Oh, grief, this—to dine alone with Vere—was something she just did not need!

It was with mixed feelings, however, that, glancing through her bedroom window when the time came for her to go and collect the twins, she saw Vere's car coming up the drive. As she watched she saw that he had parked it at the front. All too obviously he was dining somewhere that evening—she would have the dining-room to herself.

Wondering what the dickens was the matter with her that she should at first be upset at the thought that she and Vere would be sole dinner companions that evening, and then should feel quite disturbed—for the want of a better word—that she would not after all have his company, Fabienne impatiently snatched up her car keys and went charging from her room.

By her calculations, Vere should have been well clear of the hall by then, but somehow it turned out that he was neither in his study nor passing the time of day with Mrs Hobbs in her kitchen.

Fabienne spotted him the moment she glanced over the landing rail. He was below in the hall, the sound of her bedroom door closing having, it seemed, halted him and caused him to look up.

He stayed where he was and as her colour flared— God, she'd be glad when she grew out of that—she had no option but to carry on. Which she did at quite some pace. She was undecided as she drew level with the tall, dark-haired—and arrogant with it—brute, if she would speak to him or not.

However when, unspeaking, she went to go past him, a hand shot out and grabbed her shoulder. Here it comes, she thought as she stopped dead in her tracks. Either he's going to give me a lecture on how one should answer the phone when one's employer is on the other end, or I'm going to get one on the courtesies required when passing one's employer in the hall.

He turned her to face him and, as her heart chose that moment to give a wild flutter, she felt herself pinned by his fierce, direct gaze. But he took her to task neither about her telephone manner or anything else, but enquired curtly, 'Where are you off to in such a hurry?' And when, all large brown eyes, she just stared at him and obviously was not quick enough with her answers, 'Do you have some man waiting?' he grunted.

Again she felt the urge to hit him. She managed to resist that urge, however, though could not resist replying with some of the anger he could so instantly provoke. 'It's not beyond the realms of possibility that I might see Lyndon Davies where I'm going!' she snapped, her glance drawn to Vere's mouth, magnificent still, even though there was presently a look of grimness about it.

'Lyndon Davies?' he barked.

'He's the man I told you about. The one who asked me for a date when I took Kitty and John to sch——'

'You're paid to look after the twins, not to flirt with all and sundry!' he snarled before she could finish—and again her right hand itched.

'For your information,' she flared, 'Lyndon Davies is the uncle of the child whose birthday party it is today. That's where the children are—I'm on my way to collect them!'

Hostile grey eyes bored into smouldering brown ones as almost toe to toe they glared pugilistically at each other. Then, 'I'll save you the trouble. What's the address?' he rapped.

She had no idea. 'It's the only house in the village with a cluster of balloons attached to the gate-post,' she hurled at him and, as one, they turned their backs on each other.

Pig! Swine! she fumed, as she stormed back to her room. She wondered if she'd have felt better if she had belted him one. She doubted it, but oh, how she wished that she'd tried.

Kitty and John were full of the super time they'd had at the party and burst enthusiastically into the playroom to tell her all about it. As expected, neither of them wanted anything else to eat, and when she had got them a little quietened down Fabienne took them to see their mother.

Rachel was very subdued, Fabienne felt, though she made tremendous efforts to ask her offspring all the right questions about the party. And as Kitty climbed on to her mother's lap for a cuddle, Rachel made more efforts and suggested she would take care of the twins while Fabienne went and had her dinner.

She had been right, Fabienne realised, in thinking that Rachel would not be dining downstairs with her that evening. But, when it had been in her mind to have something on a tray too, Fabienne, aware of the giant efforts Rachel was making to beat her depression, suddenly saw that there came a time when one had to back off. A time when she had to stop feeling protective, and leave Rachel to cope the best she could. She would only be downstairs anyway, and then for not much longer than about half an hour.

'See you later, then,' she agreed, and returned to her own room to wash.

For some reason, though—and she owned that her thoughts had been far away on her fiend of an employer—she discovered as she went to leave her room that not only had she washed her face and applied a dab of powder and lipstick, but that she had changed as well.

Of which, as she walked into the dining-room a few minutes later, she was heartily glad. Not that her dress was the most stylish in her wardrobe, but it was long-length, of sage and cream silk, showed off her tiny waist to perfection—and was one Vere Tolladine had never seen before.

'Good evening,' she greeted him civilly, only by the skin of her teeth holding down the words. 'What are you doing here?' She had been positive he would be dining out that evening! To see him standing there over by the window as she went in had completely thrown her. 'Er—Rachel won't be down. She's had a bit of a tiny set-back,' she stated hurriedly as she fought to get herself back together again. Really—what *was* it about this man?

She saw his eyes flick over her figure without making a meal of it and saw the way he strolled back from the window and waited for her to take her seat before he took his own opposite her. That small courtesy was a mark in his favour but, if he was still in the same snarly, brutish mood of a short while ago, she might yet be deciding to eat in her room.

But, to her amazement, Vere seemed now to be in the best of humours—either that or his inbred good manners decreed a halt to hostilities while they ate. For his tone was quite affable as he remarked, 'Rachel is otherwise making such excellent progress that an occasional hiccup along the way can only be expected.'

My word! Add charm to good manners! Feeling a mite stunned, Fabienne took her seat. 'Um—the children,' she volunteered, 'they won't be down either.'

She looked across at him, and saw that he wasn't a bit fazed by that piece of information. Indeed, there was a definite gleam of amusement in those direct grey eyes that stared into her large brown ones as he commented drily, 'It's just you and me, then.'

Was he laughing at her? Was he daring to laugh at her? 'I can report sick if you like!' she assured him snappily, ready and able to be back in her room within a minute.

But, 'Stop being so prickly,' he instructed her to her astonishment—her, prickly! And, while she was still gaping at that, he picked up his knife and began on his pâté starter.

She threw him a stubborn, mulish look, which was rather wasted because he was not looking, and then, feeling slightly exasperated by this man who, as ever, was adept at disturbing her equilibrium, she picked up her knife too and, quite in the manner of 'if you can't beat 'em, join 'em', she tackled Mrs Hobbs' gorgeous home-made pâté.

Somehow, and she never knew exactly how—though she rather suspected it had something to do with the charm of her fellow diner when he forgot to be a bear—

by the time they had progressed on to the meat and veg-
etables course she discovered that her crossness with Vere
had gone. What was more, when she had always considered herself something of a private person, she suddenly woke up to the fact that they had been discussing
her for the past five minutes.

'What about you?' she attempted to put that matter
right straight away.

'Me?' There was again that hint of laughter in his
look—only, oddly, she found that she was no longer
feeling 'prickly' about it.

'I've told you my taste in literature and theatre and
that, provided my listener's tone-deaf, I'm fantastic
playing the piano, but——'

'How many years did you say you had lessons?'

'It seemed forever,' she laughed. 'Then, one superb,
wonderful day, my parents finally cottoned on that they
might just as well throw the tuition fees on the fire—
their little one was never going to make the big time.'
She halted and looked at him, all huge eyes and astonishment. 'How did you *do* that?'

'Do what?'

'You know,' she accused, but had to smile. 'You had
me talking about me again!'

He grinned, actually grinned, and she was fascinated.
'So they cancelled the music teacher and——'

'Did you have piano lessons?' She refused to talk
about herself any more.

He laughed, and looked at her smiling mouth. 'You
know you're beautiful, of course.'

Her mouth fell open in surprise. There was nothing
out of the way in his comment, nothing to get offended
about or see as a pass. It was not a pass, just something
that seemed to have fallen from his lips because, as he
looked at her, that was what he saw—and he'd said so.

'Why, thank you,' she said, trying desperately hard to take his compliment in the light way it was meant, and to ignore the ridiculous surge of joy she experienced to know that Vere thought her beautiful. 'Er...have you always been interested in finance?' she questioned lightly, in an endeavour to take his attention away from her and on to the subject he was manifestly good at—his work.

'I seem to have an aptitude for it,' he commented without boasting, then saw that her plate was empty. 'Ready for pudding?' he enquired.

Fabienne stacked their used dishes on the trolley for Mrs Hobbs to wheel out later, and accepted the helping of trifle that Vere served up for her. 'Thank you,' she murmured, and waited till he was back from the sideboard with the cheese and biscuits he favoured before she dipped her spoon into the first delicious mouthful.

Then she became aware of Vere's eyes on her and flicked a glance to him to see that, while his expression was unsmiling, there was amusement lurking in the grey depths of his eyes.

'I've a dab of cream on the end of my nose?' she suggested.

He shook his head. 'It's a delight to watch a woman eat with such total disregard for her figure.'

That brought immediately to mind the very beautiful women he must know and dine with—and she found she did not like such thoughts. 'I'm lucky,' she told him, 'I come from a long line of food-relishers who never have to diet.'

'I think you come from a long line of people who enjoy work, too,' he commented, his eyes on her lively face.

'How do you know that?' she asked in surprise.

He shrugged, his amused glance on her surprised look. 'It's fairly obvious. Your father's firm is doing well—

that doesn't happen without some very hard work from both him and your brother.' She almost butted in to say, Ah, about my brother, it was him yesterday—but, she had to own, she was much intrigued by what he was saying. What he had been able to analyse. 'The fact that where there was no need for your mother to work—from a financial point of view, she chose so to do.'

'My word, your investigators certainly did their work well when looking into my background to see if I was a safe person to be with the children,' Fabienne put in a shade coolly.

'Would you have it any other way?'

A simple question. It did not take much thinking about. 'Galling though it is,' she confessed openly, 'you're right. I'm sorry.'

Looking at him, she expected to see yet more amusement in his eyes. But, strangely, there was none. He was studying her, silently, as if—as if... arrested by something in her. She blinked, and then consigned that notion to the scrap-heap, because when she looked at him again the only studying of her she could tell was in her imagination. And his tone was totally matter-of-fact when, flicking a glance to her shiny dark hair, 'And then,' he continued, 'there's—you.'

'I come into this?' she queried, suddenly feeling quite vague as to what they had been talking about. He really did have a most wonderful mouth—the rest of him was quite terrific, too.

'We were discussing the working Prestons,' he re-minded her, and she abruptly snapped out of it. Good heavens, what on earth was she thinking about?

'Ah, yes,' she agreed.

'There was no need for you to work, either, but you chose to.'

'Well, that's true,' she allowed. 'It would never have suited me to stay at home twiddling my thumbs all day.'

'To work in your mother's gown shop was what you wanted?'

'I didn't know what I wanted when I left school. Though,' she quickly qualified, 'I did know what I did *not* want.' Vere poured her some coffee from the perspex container keeping warm on a very low burner, and glanced at her, clearly waiting to hear more. 'My father offered me the chance to train in engineering but, while my maths would have been up to it, I just didn't see myself as an engineer.'

'So you went to assist your mother.'

'As you know,' she granted.

'And when the business closed and you still felt the need to work you came to work here, luckily for us.'

Her eyes shot to him at those words 'luckily for us', but the pleasure, the joy she experienced on hearing him say he felt that—despite the fact she would stand toe to toe and argue with him if called upon so to do—was out of all proportion. Which, she all at once felt, with some confusion, left her feeling wide open.

Desperately she searched for some way to counteract that—and found it in a saucy, 'You'll have to watch that, Mr Tolladine. That's twice this evening you've paid me a compliment.'

She could see that she had amused him. Even as he told her sternly, 'You must be about the most impudent female I've ever employed,' there was no mistaking the gleam of humour in his eyes. And, his mind on the work theme, he asked seriously, 'What will you do after this assignment?'

That promptly sobered up her mood too. Somehow she did not, just then, want to contemplate leaving. 'Something, obviously, but what I'm not sure about.'

'Open another dress shop?' he suggested.

She shook her head. 'My mother's been told by her doctor to rest. Nothing life-threatening,' she quickly added. 'But...'

'But if you open a gown shop locally, your mother will find it impossible to keep away?' He at once understood.

She smiled at him for his understanding, and felt like so much jelly when he smiled back. 'As you said yourself—the Prestons are workers,' she murmured, glanced down at her coffee-cup and saw that somehow, without knowing it, she had downed the coffee he had poured her. It was time, she decided, that she went and got her head together. She dabbed at the corners of her mouth with her napkin, placed it on the table and stood up. 'I'd better go and see if the children need anything,' she murmured, about the best she could do just then in an exit line. 'Goodnight,' she said as she turned from the table—and found Vere there at the door before her.

When he did not immediately open the door for her to go through, though, she looked up at him, found he was looking down at her—and was rendered almost speechless when he quietly asked, 'Why didn't you tell me that your kissing visitor of yesterday was your brother?'

'How did you find that out?' she gasped, not certain her jaw had not dropped again.

'It wasn't difficult,' he drawled. 'In fact, so uncomplicated you wouldn't believe. On the way back Kitty and John were counting up how many had been at the party—which, my ears picked up, had included an Alex, who had the same name as Fenne's brother, who'd come to see her yesterday.'

'Ah!' Fabienne murmured as she took that on board.

'Ah, indeed,' Vere replied, and insisted, 'So tell me, why did you not tell me that the kissing you were doing yesterday was a kiss of greeting to your brother?'

'What—and risk you having a good opinion of me?' she countered saucily.

His answer was to place his hands lightly on her tiny waist while the corners of his mouth turned fascinatingly upwards. 'Did I mention that you were the most impudent of women?' he queried.

The corners of her mouth went up too. She saw his glance go to her mouth, and stay there. 'You—um—might have done,' she answered huskily, and felt her world swim when gently, unhurriedly, and giving her all the time in the world to pull away if she so desired, Vere slowly took her in his arms.

Fabienne could not have pulled away had her life depended upon it. When his mouth gently met hers, so her heart thundered so loudly she thought that he would hear it. She felt his body near to hers, and moved in closer, and, putting her arms up over his shoulders, kissed him back. It was a warm kiss, a wonderful kiss, and she never wanted it to end.

But it did end. As unhurriedly as it had started. She felt the pressure of Vere's arms about her increase then slowly their kiss broke, and slowly he took a half-step back.

There was a warm, exciting look in his eyes as he stared down into her limpid brown ones, and his voice was warm, too, when softly he murmured, 'Perhaps I'd better let you go.'

There was no perhaps about it as far as Fabienne was concerned. She had always scoffed at the old-fashioned women 'swooning' but Vere was having such an effect on her that she felt just then that if she did not go, and quickly, she might swoon straight away. She searched for some bright, brittle quip of parting, but there just wasn't one. For one of the very few times in her life she was stuck for words.

'Goodnight,' she replied, not recognising that husky voice as hers and, as miraculously she found the door open, she fled. The only thought in her head as she went hastily up to her room was, Vere Tolladine, you're just going to have to stop doing that. How could any man, so easily, so entirely without effort, make such a nonsense of her?

Fortunately—or unfortunately; Fabienne was undecided which—there was no space in which to dwell on the effect Vere Tolladine had on her over the next few days. Because firstly Kitty awoke with a headache the next day—too much excitement the day before, Fabienne rather thought—and did not want to go to school. It was one of the few mornings when Rachel was up too, if not fully awake—her thoughts most definitely elsewhere, anyhow, as she absently told Kitty that she need not go to school that day.

'If she's not going to school, I'm not going!' John declared, and from the stubborn look on his otherwise sweet little face Fabienne knew she was going to need all her tact and patience to get him there.

But, to her great surprise, she heard Rachel tell him that if he did not want to go to school then he need not. She opened her mouth to protest, but abruptly closed it. The twins had been through a lot and Rachel, their mother—not she—knew them far better than she did. If Rachel decreed that they need not go to school, who was she, at this stage of their healing development, to say a word against that?

The upshot of the whole matter, however, was that the children dawdled and would not be hurried and, by the time she had them out on the landing ready to go down to breakfast, Fabienne was in time to see Vere's departing back as he strode down the hall to the rear exit to where his car was garaged.

There followed a day when Kitty and John seemed positively to egg each other on to see who could be the most badly behaved. It was a wet day out, and they invaded the kitchen before she could stop them. But even Mrs Hobbs, who bribed them with cake and other goodies, eventually lost patience with their bickering and gave up on them.

'Some days are like that,' Fabienne apologised as she herded them out of the kitchen and racked her brains for something for them to do that would not elicit a 'don't want to' response.

By the time dinner-time that evening arrived, Fabienne was feeling very much frazzled around the edges, while Rachel was showing definite signs of being weepy.

Any hope that Vere's influence at dinner might make things better was doomed when they discovered that not only was Vere not dining with them that evening, but he was not home yet.

Some days are *definitely* like that, Fabienne mused, feeling, she had to own, a touch out of sorts when she went to bed that night. And yet, somehow, she had a feeling that it was not the children's naughty behaviour that was the cause of her 'out of sorts' feeling.

To her further surprise Rachel was again up and about early the next morning and Fabienne was put to wondering if she was trying to wean herself off her sleeping-pills. She seemed quite decisive, too, for when John this time said he had a headache, she at once stated that since it was the last day of the school week, he and Kitty might as well have that day off too. 'Mind, I want better behaviour from the pair of you today,' she warned, when Fabienne had thought she had not so much as noticed the first-class impression they had given yesterday of being two little horrors.

That Friday was not the best Friday of Fabienne's life. It started off badly in that Vere was not there at breakfast-time. And while she was certain that she did not give a hoot that, obviously, he had not been home all night—she hoped he had enjoyed himself, whoever she was—thoughts of Vere seemed to pop into her head at any idle moment throughout that day.

Not that there were many idle moments, for the children, though angelic by comparison to their behaviour yesterday, were alternately fractious and clinging.

'Do you have to go away tomorrow?' John asked her at one point, all large eyes, husky voice and heart-tearingly sad-looking.

'I'll be back Sunday evening,' she told him brightly.

'But it's not the same,' Kitty complained.

'Oh, you'll be all right,' Fabienne told them bracingly but, as the pair kept up with the same theme for what seemed like hours, she knew that it was only the fact that it was her father's special birthday on Sunday that stopped her from promising she would stay. Even Rachel, too, all sad and unhappy-eyed, seemed to be pleading with her not to go.

By then, if it were not for the fact that she intended to give her mother all the help she could on Saturday, Fabienne was sure that she would otherwise not have left Brackendale until Sunday, and for that day only. Then the phone rang and Rachel answered it, and passed it to her. 'It's for you,' she smiled, and shepherded the children from the room so that Fabienne could take her call in private.

It was her mother, ringing to remind her that it was her father's birthday. What was the matter with everyone? First Alex ringing and leaving a message with Rachel to remind her, and now her mother!

'I haven't forgotten,' Fabienne answered—and just then saw that John had sneaked back and was looking soulfully at her. Guilt clutched her conscience. 'Though——' She broke off as Rachel came and rounded John up.

'Don't say you're not coming!'

'Yes, I am, of course I am. It's just—well, the twins are having a bit of a bad day and don't want me to leave them.'

As she had so many times in the past, her mother found an instant solution. 'Then bring them with you!' she declared. 'We've heaps of room, and——'

'Oh...' Fabienne stalled. 'Rachel's unlikely to let them come without her.'

'I should think not, indeed,' Clare Preston declared stoutly, and Fabienne came away from the phone to go looking for Rachel.

It was a half an hour, though, before she could get her on her own to extend her mother's warm invitation to her. 'Oh, I don't know,' Rachel hedged, but Fabienne had seen the way her eyes had lit up at the idea.

'I'm sure you'd enjoy it,' she pressed. 'Just as I'm sure the change will do you good. But, apart from that, my family would love to have you.'

As dinner-time that evening approached the only person left to tell that he would be having his home to himself was Vere. Fabienne pondered if it was her place to tell him or if she should leave it to Rachel. But since he was her employer, and since it was to her home that they were all going—and since Rachel, with John helping, was engaged in battle with truculent Kitty on the non-packing of a pair of shocking-pink socks—

Fabienne slipped downstairs a few minutes before the others.

She found Vere in the drawing-room and, ignoring the idiotic skipped beats of her heart on seeing him there, tall, sophisticated and all man, she launched straight away into why she had sought him out—and watched as his expression went from urbane to hostile.

'You're *all* going to Lintham?' he barked harshly.

Who rattled his cage? In a split-second she was denying that her heart had ever, for the briefest of moments, skipped a beat on seeing him.

'Why not?' she challenged, sparks of defiance immediately flashing in her eyes.

'Your parents are getting on—they can't possibly want the fuss and bother of a pair of children——'

'Yes, they can!' she interrupted hotly. 'It was my mother's suggestion, as a matter of fact. Besides, it will do Rachel a power of —'

'Rachel knows of this invitation, does she?' he questioned bluntly.

'And approves!' Fabienne tossed at him crossly.

'Then far be it from me to do anything to upset your arrangements!' he grunted.

When Fabienne went to bed that night she found it just impossible to get Vere's hostile attitude out of her head. Why, though, was he so hostile about Rachel and the children leaving Brackendale for just two days and one night?

She was awake long into the night, puzzling it over. You'd have thought, bearing in mind the terrible time he'd had of it that other wet weekend, that he'd be thrilled to bits to have his home all to himself for the first time since Easter.

Perhaps, though, he'd some other outing planned for them and she, by taking them to Lintham, had messed that up? Fabienne discounted that idea as soon as it was born. If Vere Tolladine had made plans for the children that weekend, then, without a doubt, her telling him that they were all going to Lintham would have received just one answer—that answer being, 'Tough'.

So why was he opposed to Rachel and the——? Her thoughts broke off right there. And a second later she was recalling his harsh 'You're *all* going to Lintham?'— and suddenly, wretchedly, Fabienne had the answer. It was not the twins so much that he objected to having a weekend away from Brackendale—but Rachel!

Fabienne discovered she was shaken to her roots at the possibility that Vere was in love with his stepbrother's widow but, as such thoughts plagued her for most of the next morning, she could find no other explanation.

Vere was not about when they left for Lintham, where they were warmly received by Fabienne's parents. Fabienne entered into the generally jolly atmosphere, but the whole while she could not stop thinking of Vere. Was his love for Rachel the main reason why he had taken Rachel and her children to live at Brackendale, and not, as she'd thought, because his sensitivity, his sense of responsibility was such that there had been no way he could leave them muddling on, clearly not coping, in the situation he'd found them that Easter.

Alex and his son Philip came to stay on Saturday afternoon and Alex it was, after a glance at Rachel's pale features, who suggested a walk of discovery in the fields and lanes that were close by his parents' property.

'I don't think...' Rachel began.

'You won't need a coat,' Alex smiled. 'I'm sure it won't rain. Where's your lead, Oliver?' he addressed the ever hopeful Jack Russell.

Because there was quite a bit of preparing still to do for tomorrow's lunch party, Fabienne stayed behind. An hour went by, and then two, and a short while later a happy band of walkers and discoverers returned.

Fabienne was delighted to see that Rachel had a hint of colour to her face, but felt that she might need her own space for a while. As, apparently, so too did her mother, for it was with a wealth of compassionate tact that she suggested, 'If you'd like to go upstairs and rest for a while, my dear...'

Rachel had gone up to her room and Fabienne was alone in the kitchen a short while later when her brother came in. 'Fenne,' he said, and she knew that tone.

'You want something?' she teased accusingly—but saw, instead of laughing, that he was deadly serious.

'I want to take Rachel out to dinner, but she says she can't because it would be too much of a cheek to expect you to keep an eye on Kitty and John at weekends as well as in the week.'

To say that she felt shattered by this most unexpected development was an understatement. But Alex was her brother and she loved him dearly—and she could not think beyond that at this moment.

'*Bon appetit*—with my blessing,' she grinned and Alex went whistling out of the kitchen.

Five minutes later Tom Walton phoned. 'Seems years since I saw you, Fenne.' It was two weeks. 'Can you come out to play tonight?'

'If I can bring a pair of seven-year-olds with me—and an eight-year-old,' she added for good measure, with no intention of going out anywhere.

'In the words of the bard—stuff that, Juliet! What are you doing tomorrow?'

Fabienne laughed, turned him down for tomorrow too, and went back to her chores—and back to her thoughts

of how, ever since yesterday evening when she had gone
to see Vere, her head had been bombarded with one
startling thought after another.

If asked, she would have sworn that neither her brother
nor Rachel were remotely interested in keeping company
with the opposite sex yet. Yet Alex had asked, and Rachel
had accepted.

But Fabienne discovered, after Alex and Rachel had
gone, that her surprises for the day were not yet over.
Kitty, John and Philip were safely tucked up in bed, her
father was watching television—his chores for the day
completed—and she was finishing off the preparations
in the kitchen with her mother, when she thought to
thank her parent for inviting Rachel and the children
that weekend.

'I probably would have invited them anyway,' her
mother replied—and added to Fabienne's astonishment,
'But in actual fact it was Alex who suggested I should
do so.'

'*Alex* did?'

'I know,' her mother agreed. 'But isn't it wonderful
that, after all the hurt and suffering he went through
with Victoria and the divorce, he now seems to be getting
over it?'

Fabienne went to bed that night feeling more mixed-
up than ever. Vere? Vere and Rachel? Rachel and Alex?
Her head ached.

The party for her father the next day was all that it
should have been. He was happy. 'You shouldn't have!'
he protested at the gold cufflinks Fabienne gave him.

'Yes, I should,' she laughed, and hugged and kissed
him as did most everyone else.

His brothers and sisters-in-law, cousins and friends,
all arrived mid-morning for a celebratory drink and,

although some of them afterwards left, it was still a large party who sat down—later than planned—to lunch.

Mrs Cooper, their daily, came in unusually on a Sunday to help out, but even so, with Rachel and Alex helping, it was getting on for eight by the time the dishes were washed, put away and the house anywhere near back to rights.

Strangely, when Fabienne had always loved her home, she experienced an almost overwhelming anxiety to get back to Brackendale. And very near panicked when her mother suggested that, because of the lateness of the hour they should stay another night.

'Kitty and John have to be at school tomorrow,' Rachel declined, though seemed as reluctant to go as the twins looked.

'We'd better go,' Fabienne suggested, relieved that they *were* going, but now anxious to be on their way.

Goodbyes were said, and as Fabienne set the car in motion her emotions had never been more turbulent. She had seen the way Alex had seemed to be in earnest conversation with Rachel a time or two, and also on saying goodbye.

Had Alex fallen for Rachel? Had Rachel fallen for him? She wanted that neither of them should be hurt again. And, oh, lord, what about Vere?

Fabienne had driven through the village of Sutton Ash, and was on the drive of Brackendale when she realised, most particularly, that she did not want Vere to be hurt. Oh, grief, she thought, and steered her car round to the rear and pulled up.

Because of the time Rachel did not hang around with the children but, leaving Fabienne to put the car away, collected up their gear and went straight into the house.

The car was garaged and Fabienne had her overnight bag in one hand, the garage door key in the other when, hearing a sound, she spun round from the garage—and met the glare of Vere Tolladine's grey eyes full on.

And then she knew. It was not Brackendale so much that she had been desperate to get back to, but its owner. It was Vere she had missed, not his home. Only then, on seeing him again, did Fabienne acknowledge what had been there all the time—that she was in love with him.

Which was a great pity. Because in a voice that was far from loving towards her—in fact in a voice that assured her he felt nothing for her whatsoever save fury— Vere Tolladine positively roared, 'What the *hell* do you think you're doing bringing those two mites home at this time of night!'

Fabienne stared helplessly at him. From somewhere, she knew, she was going to have to find some stiffening—that, or let him wipe the floor with her.

CHAPTER SEVEN

SHE was not, Fabienne decided on that instant, the type to let anyone wipe the floor with her. So, regardless of how her heart ached just to see him, she mentally drew herself up to her full height and, maybe when she should have tried to be a small degree conciliatory, 'A late night occasionally never hurt anyone!' she tossed at him.

Vere did not care for her standing up to him now any more than he had before; she could tell that from the way his mouth firmed, and the way he looked as if he could cheerfully throttle her. 'Those children are seven years old,' he reminded her harshly, 'and have to be up for school in the morning.'

'They will be up for school—I'll personally see to it!' she snapped.

'And I suppose you'll personally cope with their ill-humour, their aggression brought on by tiredness, too!'

'I've done it before!' She refused to be shouted down. 'And anyway,' she sped on, before he could get another word in, 'I've coped with your ill-humour, your aggression without too much trouble, so——'

'You insufferable, impertinent . . .' Words seemed to fail him.

'Baggage?' she supplied.

'Why the hell I put up with you, I don't know!' he roared.

'The feeling's mutual!' she hurled straight back—though took a hasty step to one side when Vere took a 'God give me strength' kind of indrawn breath and moved, his arms coming up, towards her. 'Don't you

121

dare hit me!' she yelled in panic, fairly certain then that he was about to either beat her or strangle the life out of her.

Abruptly, as her panicky words reached him, he stopped. And hostile wasn't the word for it then when, 'Get out of my sight—fast!' he thundered.

For once in her life Fabienne was pleased to obey an order without further comment. She went, and quickly!

Up in her room she closed the door and leant against it, and swallowed—hard. It was then that she discovered that she was shaking from her encounter with Vere. She took a fractured breath and, knowing that there was no way she was going to sleep, she went and sank down into her bedroom chair. Oh, God help her, this was dreadful! Would Vere really have set about her?

An hour later she had calmed down sufficiently to re-alise that, although it was probably on the cards that Vere might have caught hold of her the better to ram home his point of view—whatever that point of view was—he was probably as appalled as she at the notion that he might physically have set about her.

Another hour passed during which she acknowledged that being in love was hell. It gave you, freely and un-asked for, the sick pain of jealousy, the confusion of not knowing where the devil you were and the bewil-dering, wild, emotions of wanting only to be loving and gentle—while at the same time it let loose a veritable virago in your mouth. It was no use wondering what in creation was the matter with her—she knew. She was in love with the cantankerous swine!

For a further age Fabienne sat there, sleep light-years away, and it was only when she moved her position and caught sight of her watch and, startled, saw that it was ten-past three, that she realised that if she did not want to feel like a piece of limp rag in a few hours' time she had better try to get some sleep.

She was wide awake still, though, and thought that perhaps a shower might help her to relax. It did not, and she was in bed but still wide awake when dawn started to filter across the night sky.

When she did finally become drowsy and succumb, she was aware of not a sound. That was until *some* sound brought her slowly to the surface. She still had her eyes closed when that sound came again. It was the sound of an all-male voice—a voice she would know anywhere as it repeated, 'Fabienne!'

At once her eyes shot open. But for a moment, as her eyes registered the tall, all-masculine Vere Tolladine standing there, she had no idea where she was. 'What...?' she gasped helplessly.

'Excuse me for barging in,' Vere drawled, not looking in the least apologetic, 'but I thought someone ought to come and check that you hadn't died in the night.'

Her head suddenly cleared and with it came the reality of where she was, and who he was, and that today was Monday. 'What time is it?' she questioned huskily, and was not at all surprised to find that her voice was husky. This might be reality, but it still seemed unreal somehow.

Her question was straightforward, but his answer threw her into the wildest depths of confusion for, his voice unhurried, he took his glance from her tousled hair and dainty features and, with a meaningful glance at her bosom, 'Time you covered yourself up, I'd suggest,' he replied.

Her glance followed his and she just could not believe that when she *always*—but always—slept with the duvet up around her ears, she had for once been so restless in her sleep that the duvet, while covering one shoulder and one breast, had moved in the hours of sleep she had managed. What was more, somehow—and she was too stupefied to wonder how—the strap of her thin cotton nightdress was somewhere down her arm and now, in full view of Vere's not uninterested gaze, was one naked and beautifully rounded, pink-tipped breast.

'Oh!' she cried in horror, and was in such a panicky rush to get herself covered up that the whole of the duvet looked like ending up on the floor. 'If you were a gentleman, you'd help!' she wailed, and righted the cover, aware that her face must be as scarlet as her entire body felt.

'If you were a lady I'd——' Vere began to mock. But suddenly, as he looked at her flushed face and noted her panicky, agitated manner, so he broke off and, all mockery gone, his tone grew more astounded than anything. 'Good God!' he exclaimed. 'You *are* a virgin!'

Fabienne was by then sitting up and, with the duvet now hugged up over her shoulders and safely tucked in, so she began to feel a touch more confident. It was in the sparky manner of the old Fabienne Preston, anyhow, that she told him in no uncertain terms, 'At the risk of getting the sack—clear off!'

His answer was to grin. A huge, very pleased and amused grin—and suddenly Fabienne was feeling a whole lot better. I love you, she thought, and somehow, just at that moment, it seemed right that it should be so. He was affable, friendly—and as she looked at him it registered that he was immaculately suited, clearly about to leave for his office.

'What time *is* it?' she repeated, more urgently this time, the reality that she had slept right through her normal waking time, that she had overslept, starting to sink in.

'You know that cocky bit about the children being up for school and how you were personally going to see to it?' Vere asked, high amusement still lurking in his eyes. 'Well—you missed it.'

'Oh, grief,' she groaned and, while she loved him the more that he could refer to their set-to last night without rancour, she all but hopped out of bed then and there— but remembered. 'Er—if you wouldn't mind,' she hinted, sufficiently chastened to amend her previous 'clear off' slightly.

'Have a lie-in,' he suggested, making not the smallest move in the direction of the door.

'Kitty and John, they'll...'

'Be deep into their schoolwork by now, I shouldn't wonder.'

She started to relax. 'You've already taken them to school?' she guessed. And, when he nodded, she had the craziest notion that he had returned just to see her. 'You came back?' she queried, her voice again gone husky.

He studied her for some long moments, his eyes roving her face, her clear skin. But when he spoke Fabienne realised just what a cloud-cuckoo-land she must be in to think for a moment that, just as she wanted to see him, Vere in return wanted to see her. For his tone was the most casual when he replied, 'I forgot my briefcase.' To her joy, though, he did not at once go on his way but, with a flick of a glance to his watch as if to say he could spare her another minute, he came and parked himself on the end of her bed and enquired, 'Do anything special over the weekend?'

'We had a special birthday party for my father on Sunday,' she answered.

'So Kitty told me. She and John got on well with your nephew Philip by the sound of it.'

'They did. They——'

'What about Saturday?'

'They——' she began.

'They went for a walk—and can they have a dog like Oliver.'

'Oops,' she laughed. 'I'm sorry.'

'Think nothing of it,' he returned, the corners of his mouth starting to pick up. 'So what did *you* do on Saturday?' he questioned, clearly having heard in a very short while all that the twins had been up to.

'I stayed home, and——' Abruptly she broke off. She had been about to mention that her brother had taken Rachel out to dinner but all of a sudden she felt sensitive that Vere might be hurt if he knew that.

'And what?' he demanded, the hint of a smile on his mouth coming to nothing.

'You want to be bored?'

'So bore me.'

'So I stayed home and peeled potatoes and folded napkins prettily, and...'

'No boyfriend?'

'I did get an offer, but he wouldn't take the twins as well.'

Vere's right eyebrow ascended but she again saw humour come to his eyes. 'The man's a complete cad!' he observed drily, and she loved him so much and wanted to laugh—but he was going on. 'So, although you were supposedly off duty, you still felt a strong sense of responsibility for Kitty and John.'

'They were my guests.'

'Which means,' Vere began, his look steady on her warm brown eyes, 'that you worked all weekend.'

Just to have him this pleasant to her, this charming, wiped out every memory of how hostile he could be when he felt like it. But, with her backbone already feeling like so much water, Fabienne struggled with all she had to hide her inner feelings.

'Oh, I wouldn't call it work,' she answered, and damned, as Vere stared thoughtfully at her, the fact that her voice was still husky.

'I suppose,' he mused out loud, 'that if I were halfway towards being a decent employer I'd offer you time off in lieu.'

No! She did not want that! On the one hand it was a tremendous relief that it was not the husky tone of her voice or the emotions in her over him, which he'd seen and been thoughtful about, but on the other hand she wanted to see more and more of him, to be with him— albeit with others. She would positively loathe time off in lieu!

'Nobody——' she found a grin to toss his way '—could accuse you of that.'

'Ye gods—did I call you cocky?' he retorted, his eyes on the impish curve to her mouth.

Her grin widened—then all at once her heart started to pound for all it was worth. Because suddenly Vere stood up, left the end of her bed, and seemed to come closer. If he kisses me I've no resistance, she panicked, half in need, half in fear of yet giving herself away.

But, just to show how mindless she had become in her love for him, Vere showed not the smallest likelihood to kiss her, but instead took another quick glance to his watch and, remarking, 'Must away to earn a crust,' he went striding to the door.

Fabienne sat just where she was for some minutes after he had gone—had Vere really come to her bedroom? Had she and Vere really had that conversation just now— she in her bed and he sitting on the end of it, all business-suited and ready to go to his business?

Fabienne got out of bed and headed for the shower to get ready to start her day. Yes, it had happened—and a smile came to her mouth as she recalled the way he had thrown back at her her 'They will be up for school—I'll personally see to it'. She had deserved that. Though, considering the time it must have been when she had eventually closed her eyes, perhaps it was not so surprising that she had overslept. She must have slept soundly, too, for if the children had tiptoed in to see her then she had not heard them. The first sound she had heard had been the voice of the man she loved calling her name.

She was not the only one up late that morning, she discovered. Although she could remember days when Rachel had not surfaced at all—or at any rate not shown her face. She met Rachel on the landing as they both left their rooms.

'I'm late!' Rachel exclaimed at once. 'After promising myself that I was not going to stay in bed a minute past eight ever again, I did it again.'

'Don't worry about it—I was late myself this morning,' Fabienne smiled, and went down the stairs with Rachel, all at once overwhelmingly glad that Rachel had assumed that, late or not, she had been up in time to take the children to school that morning. For she suddenly knew that she did not want to tell Rachel anything of Vere's visit to her room. It was private, and beautiful, and if love had made her a miser then so be it, but she just did not want to share it with anyone.

Rachel seemed pensive over breakfast, she thought, though Fabienne was pleased to see that she had bothered with her hair and had applied a small amount of makeup—a vast difference from the 'far-away' woman she had been not so very many short weeks ago.

'Anything in particular you'd like to do today?' Fabienne enquired as they drank their coffee.

'I——' Rachel began, when just then the phone rang. Rachel did not move, and Fabienne was nearer to it.

She discovered it was Alex on the other end. 'Did I forget something?' she asked, having seen him not twenty-four hours ago, and, as fear abruptly struck, 'Are Mum and Dad OK?'

'Fine, fine,' he assured her straight away and gave her more to think about than he knew when he went on, 'I don't suppose Rachel's around, is she?'

'Rachel's here with me now. Did you want to...?'

'Can I have a word?'

Fabienne was glad she had her back to Rachel, but managed to cover the surprise that hit her by quipping in sisterly fashion, 'Don't work too hard,' and with that she turned round to Rachel. 'Alex wants a word,' she said, and held out the phone.

Without saying anything Rachel left her chair. 'Thanks,' she offered as she took the phone from her. 'Hello,' Fabienne heard her say down the phone. Then, 'Fine. How are you? Really?' And, with nothing being said to indicate her presence was needed, Fabienne made herself scarce. This was obviously a personal call.

Fabienne's head was buzzing with the whys and the wherefores, and the implications she saw in her brother telephoning especially to speak privately to Rachel.

First and foremost she did not want Alex to be hurt, she thought as she went upstairs to collect her bag. There was no way that she could stand by and watch him suffer again, she fretted as, downstairs again, she passed the breakfast-room where Rachel and her brother were still in telephone conversation.

And what about Vere? she thought as she went and unlocked her garage. A whole conglomeration of 'if this, if that' was rocking her as she backed out her car. Vere most of all, more than her dearly loved brother even, she could not bear to be hurt.

And what about Rachel? she worried, as she halted her car on the standing area and sorted out some of the debris that Kitty and John had managed to leave in the back during the car ride home yesterday. It was true, as she'd owned only that morning, that Rachel appeared to be coming out of her depression. But... Fabienne's thoughts slid quickly back to Vere again. Oh, she couldn't bear it if he was the one to be hurt. But then, what of Alex? What of Rachel?

With her head chasing around in the same agitated circles, Fabienne suddenly realised that, whatever happened, there was absolutely nothing that she could do about it. But, from what she could see, of a certainty someone was going to get hurt.

She tried to tell herself that she was making a mountain out of a molehill. Alex had only been out with Rachel once, for goodness' sake. And one date and the odd phone-call did not make a full-blown relationship, did it? Even if it was true that Rachel was the first female she knew whom Alex had shown an interest in since his divorce.

Fabienne was just thinking of how her brother must have been the first man Rachel had dated since her husband, when Rachel came looking for her.

'Shall we go for a walk?' Rachel asked.

'Good idea,' Fabienne responded, but could not help but notice the strange mood Rachel was in throughout the walk—one moment silent and pensive, the next her speech jerky, her manner restless.

They returned to Brackendale for a snack lunch, but it was a bit of a wasted effort because neither of them had any appetite. Though Rachel did surprise her as they returned to the drawing-room by going to move nomadically to stare out of the window, from where she announced, 'I think I'm going to sell my house.'

'Oh?' Fabienne queried, hiding the jolt of surprise to
hear that—part of her delighted that Rachel was at last
showing signs of wanting to make her own decisions,
while another part of her wondered if Rachel was intending to move into Brackendale *permanently*.

'I know now that I shall never want to live there again,'
Rachel went on. 'I've lived here; I've been in your
home—suddenly everything I had with Nick seems
sullied, sordid—and nothing to do with me, the person
I know I am deep down.'

By the sound of it, Rachel feared she had been in
danger of accepting the sordid standards of her womaniser of a husband, and had let her own higher standards drop. 'If I can help at all?' she offered, unable to
fault the notion that for Rachel's own sake it might benefit her to get rid of the home which her dead husband
had sullied by taking his mistress there.

'Thanks, Fabienne—I might take you up on that.'

Rachel then seemed to go into her shell again so that
where her thoughts went Fabienne had no idea. She went
with her to pick the children up from school, though,
and when Lyndon Davies somehow separated them she
went on ahead with the children while Lyndon invited
Fabienne to go with him to a jazz concert in Haychester
that evening.

Fabienne liked jazz, but knew better than to confess
it. 'Some other time,' she smiled, and left him to go and
catch Rachel up.

Because Mrs Hobbs had mentioned how dreadfully
she had missed seeing the children at the weekend,
Fabienne and Rachel left them with her to have tea in
the kitchen while they returned to the drawing-room.
Rachel was restless again, Fabienne noticed, and her tone
was jerky again, too, when, as if determined to be more
decisive than she had been in the recent past, she jumped

up and, going over to the window, declared, 'Perhaps it's time I went and made my peace with my parents.'

'Perhaps it might be a good idea,' Fabienne agreed slowly, as Rachel turned to her.

'I...' Rachel hesitated. 'I need to think!' she said rather desperately—and Fabienne knew that she could not help her there. From where she was viewing it, it seemed to her that Rachel was in something of a panic because there were two men showing an interest in her—Vere and Alex—and Fabienne just could not say a word. Then she found that she had no need to because suddenly Rachel had swung agitatedly back to the window and, 'Here's Vere!' she cried. And while Fabienne's insides became a jumbled, excited mass that Vere was not only home but home early, Rachel, with more energy than she had seen her use, was exclaiming, 'I must see him!' and had dashed out.

Indeed, so fast did Rachel move that as Fabienne got to the window she saw that the other woman was out on the drive before Vere could steer his car round to the rear—if that had been his intention.

Fabienne took a step back so that she could not be seen, but that did not prevent her from being able to observe the way that Vere halted his car, exchanged a few words with Rachel, and then got out of his car and stood with his stepsister-in-law on the drive in what looked like very earnest conversation.

In her heart Fabienne knew that she should not be watching, unseen, these two people in such private conversation. But she seemed powerless to look away. That was until suddenly Vere put an arm about Rachel's shoulders—and a knife went through Fabienne. She stayed watching only a moment longer, but when Vere said something and looked down to Rachel and smiled—

and Rachel smiled back—she just could not take any more.

She was up in her room barely knowing that she had moved. She hurt. She wanted to leave. But—a shuddery kind of breath escaped her—she could not leave. How could she?

Suddenly Fabienne realised that she could not say with absolute honesty why it was that she could not leave. Was it that she felt that Kitty and John needed her, or that Rachel needed her? Or was it Vere—who did not need her and never would—whom she could not leave?

That thought wounded her pride and made her ashamed that she should be so pathetic. Which, in turn, fired her to think that, when she might not be able to leave so easily, there was just no way she was going to sit at the same dinner table as both Rachel and Vere that evening.

With that knowledge came the knowledge also that she was going to draw too much attention to herself unless she had a very good reason for not going down to dinner that evening. She thought of her conversation with Vere—in this very room—this morning, and, fiercely turning her thoughts away from how wonderful that time had been, she forced herself to remember only what Vere had said about her having time off in lieu of the time she had put in over the weekend. Normally she would not have given time off another thought. But she was hurting, hurting like crazy, and she was taking the evening off. Between them, he and Rachel could supervise the twins.

There was no telephone directory in her room but there was an extension, and she was too upset just then to want to go down the stairs looking for a telephone directory and so risk bumping into Vere. And upset enough not to give a damn if directory enquiries charged ten times the amount they did for looking up the telephone number she wanted.

A few minutes later and she was speaking with Dilys Bragg. 'Is Lyndon there?' she enquired after a few pleasantries.

'You *can* come to the jazz concert?' he asked, before he had even said hello.

'Not only that—I'll treat you to dinner in Haychester first,' she replied. Though qualified, 'But I'd like to go in my car.'

'That's good,' Lyndon returned. 'I haven't got one.'

Fabienne put down the phone wondering how it could be that, when she felt as if she was bleeding inside, she could at the same time smile at Lyndon Davies' banter. She was not, however, feeling much like smiling when a few seconds afterwards her inherent good manners came and tripped her up and decreed she would have to go downstairs anyway. Courtesy, not to mention the respect she had for Mrs Hobbs, demanded that she go and tell her that she would not be in for dinner.

Still, it was only because she was certain that by now Vere would be either in his own room or closeted, the door closed, in the drawing-room with his evening paper, that Fabienne tripped lightly down the stairs. She was passing by the study door, though, when she realised that she had badly miscalculated. For the door opened and there, direct grey-eyed and absolutely marvellous, stood Vere!

She went to speed on, but suddenly she felt his hand on her arm as he spun her round. At once everything in her went haywire. His touch was electric! She hated him and loved him all at the same time, and too late realised that she should have been ready for this moment—this meeting. As it was, she was not ready, in fact she had never been more unready, and she had no idea how she should act.

This morning everything had been light and pleasant between them, but this evening—well, this evening she was feeling so out of control emotionally that she could cheerfully have either thrown herself at him or physically attacked him.

Fortunately Vere was the first to speak and saved her from making regretted choices. 'Just where are you dashing off to?' he wanted to know, his tone light, teasing almost.

He dropped his hold on her arm, and she was glad about that. She found her voice. 'I want to see Mrs Hobbs,' she answered evenly.

'And I,' he took up smoothly, 'wanted to see you.'

Crazily her heart just did not listen to her head that insisted he could mean nothing personal by that statement. But, while her heart danced Latin American, 'Oh, yes?' she enquired, quite astonished at the evenness of her tone—how could it be so when she was shaking like a leaf inside?

'Rachel tells me she wants to visit her parents tomorrow and would like to stay for a couple of days. I've encouraged her in this, but realise it will fall heavily on you.'

Some of her pain eased. But that ease was only momentary. It could have been that Rachel had rushed out to see Vere to tell him she had decided to go to her parents, and it could have been that he had put his arm about her shoulders in a gesture of the encouragement he had spoken of. But—somehow—Fabienne just knew that there was more to it than that. She just *knew* it.

But she tried to concentrate on what he was saying. 'By falling heavily on me I assume you mean that Rachel won't be taking the children with her?' she worked out aloud.

'Driving her car any distance after not driving for some while will call for all the concentration she can muster. Besides which, Kitty and John have just taken a couple of days off school. In my view a little regular routine in their lives at this stage wouldn't come amiss.'

'If you say so,' she replied, of the opinion that he was probably right but, even as he gave her a sharp look, stubbornly refusing to let him think she agreed with everything he said.

'Which leaves me asking if you would mind looking after the twins until Rachel returns.'

'Of course I will,' she replied without hesitation. 'I can take a couple of days off work and help if——'

'Grief—that's not necessary!' she exclaimed as she tried to ignore that treacherous part of her that wanted nothing more than that he should take a couple of days off work—perhaps they could go for long walks together or... 'The children will be at school most of the time anyway,' she rushed on lest she even now begged him to stay away from his office. 'And anyhow,' she hurried on, 'to look after the children was what you engaged me to do.'

'So I did,' he replied, but suddenly there was a stiff edge in his voice, and Fabienne knew then and there that never again would she share with him the affability of that morning. She knew it without doubt when, as though to dismiss her, he added arrogantly, 'You'd better go and see Mrs Hobbs about whatever it is—she'll be busy with cooking dinner and won't have t——'

'Actually,' Fabienne butted in, not liking him nor his arrogant manner one tiny bit, 'it's to tell Mrs Hobbs that I won't be in to dinner that——'

'You're eating out?' Vere rapped before she could finish.

'That was the general idea!' she flared.

'Who with?' he snarled.

'What do you mean, who with?'

'While you're under my roof, I'm resp——'

'No, you're not!'

'Who with?' he repeated aggressively.

'I've a date!' She refused to tell him.

'For the security of this house, *and* its vulnerable occupants, I insist on knowing who it is who's coming calling!' he rasped.

'He's not coming calling!' she snapped.

'You're meeting him in Haychester?'

'I'm picking him up.'

'That's a new twist!' he barked and, brilliant with his guesswork, 'Lyndon Davies!' he challenged.

'The very same!' she exploded, inwardly fuming that, despite her efforts, he knew the name of her date.

'Come home at a reasonable hour!' he ordered.

'Or you'll lock me out?' she challenged.

His hands came up to her upper arms and bit deep. 'My God, you ask for trouble!' he grated, but gained control enough to let go of her and take a step back when, his voice as cutting as cold steel, 'Have the courtesy to come in quietly,' he clipped, and disappeared into his study, closing the door on her with a determined, controlled quietness—and Fabienne only just held down a dry sob. Oh, why did she have to go and fall in love with him?

CHAPTER EIGHT

THE jazz was good, the dinner was good—but Lyndon Davies was not Vere. Lyndon, however, while it had to be said he did attempt to kiss her, took her rebuff in friendly fashion and otherwise enjoyed the evening.

'Darn it, I just knew you wouldn't run out of petrol!' he complained when Fabienne dropped him off at his sister's home.

'See you at school tomorrow morning,' she laughed, and went on her way.

It was just gone midnight as she drew up at the rear of Brackendale. She had half expected that she would be locked out, but not only was the outside light left on for her but the lock yielded to her key.

She would have gone in silently anyway but, as bidden, she went quietly along the hall, only to feel her insides somersault when she saw that the study door was open, and that there was a light shining from within. Her footsteps faltered. Vere was working in there, she just knew it! And while part of her heart went out to him that at gone midnight he was still working, she at the same time part wondered if he was purposely waiting up to see what time she arrived home.

Any anger that thought brought, though, was at once negated by the realisation that, poor darling, since the house still had to be secured for the night, what else could he do but wait up?

Fabienne did not like the feeling of being selfish but, as she stopped by the study door, it was on the tip of her tongue to apologise. That was until she met the arctic ice of Vere's look full-on, and then she would have cut her tongue out sooner than say sorry for keeping him from his bed. Without uttering a single solitary word, she went on. He, she noted, had nothing to say to her either.

As matters turned out, she did not see Lyndon Davies at the school the next morning for the simple reason that Rachel, in her ever more successful recovery, took the children to school herself.

'I thought I'd get off fairly early to go to my parents,' she explained to Fabienne, 'so I can drop Kitty and John off on my way through.'

Vere had already left for his office when Fabienne waved Rachel and the children off. She wished that she could dislike Rachel, but she could not. Somehow, regardless that Vere seemed to be taking more than step-brother-in-law interest in her, Fabienne still liked her. In a very short time, she owned, she had grown fond of them all. Wasn't it just her luck that, most of all, she had grown the fondest of the head of the household?

She went back into the house and went up to her room. She had the whole day, until it was time to collect the children, stretching out in front of her.

Restlessly she prowled her room, tidying up here and there and trying not to think. What she would really have liked to do was to get into her car and drive for miles and miles. But she took her responsibilities where Kitty and John were concerned very seriously. In the absence of their mother and their step-uncle, she felt she should stay in the vicinity of Sutton Ash. With children one never knew; one of them might develop a headache or some such and want to be brought home.

Fabienne left her room and went to check on the children's rooms, but Ingrid was already at work in there. With nothing better to do and all day to do it in, she returned to her room. It was still only ten o'clock. She went to take a look out of the window—and recognised her brother's car turning into the drive.

Grief, he'd been up early if he'd got business this way. She hurried down the stairs to meet him. 'Alex!' she exclaimed, as always pleased to see him. 'You've remembered who serves the best coffee in town.'

He grinned, and welcomed a cup. But they were in the drawing-room sharing a pot of coffee when Fabienne realised that, unusually for him, Alex seemed a touch fidgety. Though, before she could ask him if there was anything wrong, it seemed that Alex could contain himself no longer for, mid-sentence about something else, he suddenly blurted out, 'Is Rachel not down yet?'

'R——' Fabienne swallowed down her surprise. She knew her brother—this was not just an idle question. Everything about him said it was not—his serious manner, just everything! 'I'm sorry if you particularly wanted to see her—she's gone to visit her parents for a few days. Did you especially want to see her?'

He shook his head, but slowly, and to her surprise, confessed, 'I never expected to ever feel this way again. Yet, because of what both Rachel and I have been through, I've been trying to exercise caution—so what the deuce do I think I'm doing by coming here to see her today? God help me, I've fallen for her.'

'Oh, Alex. Does—does she know?'

'I think so,' he answered. 'But, just as I feel that she is feeling something of the same for me, because of our previous love partners I think we're both a bit wary.'

'But—you felt you just had to see her?' Fabienne asked carefully.

'Crazy, isn't it?' Alex acknowledged, and stood up. 'When's Rachel coming back—or, better still, have you got her parents' address? I know they live not too far away from Lintham, but not exactly where.'

'You're going to call on her at her parents'?' Fabienne exclaimed.

'Nothing so tactless.' Alex gave a half-smile. 'I might give her a ring, though, and if she fancies a drive or dinner...'

He left it there and all Fabienne felt she could do was to be as supportive as possible. He was, after all, a very special brother. 'Which makes it just as well that, while I don't have her parents' address, Rachel did happen to leave me their telephone number,' she smiled.

Fabienne watched him drive away and spent the hours until it was time to collect the children from school in wishing that she could get rid of her feeling of treachery. She had had to give Alex that telephone number, she knew that she had. But for Vere's sake she equally knew that she should not have done so.

Unhappily she walked down to the village to meet the children out of school, feeling hurt inside with the knowledge that if Rachel and Alex were going to get together then it was going to be Vere who would get hurt.

Oh, what a tangled mess! It was not as though she wanted Vere and Rachel to become an item—because she knew that she did not want Vere to marry Rachel—but she did not want him hurt, either.

'Fancy *me* taking *you* out to dinner on Saturday?' Lyndon Davies asked the moment he saw her. 'Your car, of course.'

She liked him, and smiled. 'Would that I could, Lyndon, but I'm otherwise engaged.'

'Lucky blighter! How about——?'

'Here's Kitty,' she cut through what he was saying, gave him a cheery wave, and kept up a surface cheerfulness with the children all the way home.

'Is it Thursday that Mummy comes home?' Kitty asked as they neared the gates of Brackendale—and Fabienne realised that, although Rachel had been unable to be much of a parent to her because of her illness, there was nevertheless a strong bonding between the two and Kitty was already missing her.

'That's right, but the time will fly, you'll see,' she answered brightly and, with an arm round the shoulders of both Kitty and John, 'Let's sing a song,' she suggested.

They were singing in happy, unconcerned discord as they swung into the gates and tramped down the drive. And were in fine voice as they turned the corner to the rear of the house. Then all three stopped dead.

'Uncle!' the twins exclaimed in excited unison, and Fabienne's heart started to pound to beat the band. For Vere, home early, stood there and had obviously been listening to them singing their heads off.

Oh, Vere, how I love you, Fabienne mourned, her heart going out to him. He had never seemed more dear to her than at that moment.

But alarm shot through her suddenly. Because, while she was half aware that the twins were somehow no longer sheltered by her arms but by his—where she wanted to be—Fabienne also became aware that Vere's gaze was on nobody but her!

Immediately—she panicked. Oh, God, how had she been looking at him? Had he seen something of her caring for him in her look?

She need not have worried, she realised a moment later, because as she prepared to give him the cold shoulder treatment—and so disprove any hint he might have gleaned that she was head over heels in love with him—Vere took his gaze from her and, just as if she did not exist, confided in John, 'I think Mrs Hobbs has been baking biscuits.'

With a whoop the two children set off and, as a feeling of being redundant attacked, Fabienne began to feel a shade mutinous. To his credit Vere did stand back to allow her to precede him through the door that Kitty and John had just charged through. But, with her nose in the air, she did not thank him for it.

And I'll bet that crushed him, she thought self-mockingly up in her room, knowing for certain that he was not even aware of her. She sighed, and made herself think of the children. They would both be missing their mother, not just Kitty. She went into the playroom and was there ready when, fed and refreshed, they came hurrying up the stairs.

Dinner that evening was uneventful but just as she and the children were leaving the dining-room Vere called her back.

'Yes?' she enquired, her heartbeats quickening as she looked at him. She wished with all she had that she did not love him, but knew the futility of that.

'Perhaps, when you've Kitty and John settled for the evening, you'd come down to the drawing-room.'

Her heart lurched—just him, just her. 'Very well,' she said coolly, and went on her way. Regardless that that 'perhaps' might have made it sound like an invitation, it was, she knew, an order. But, even while she admitted that taking orders was not her strong suit, her heart was singing.

She would, of course, guard against Vere seeing how she felt about him—pride, if nothing else, demanded that. But she so ached to see him, to be with him—even if he only wanted to see her to tell her off about any number of things she, who was not perfect, could have done.

In the way of all things frustrating, Kitty and John took longer to settle that night. Even while she desperately wanted to hurry them up the sooner to be with Vere, though, Fabienne somehow managed to appear as though she had all the time in the world to listen to their troubles. Especially tonight, when they did not have the security of their mother being under the same roof.

Eventually, however, she was able to leave them, Kitty in one room and John right next door. And that was when everything rose up in Fabienne and she owned that she was a dithering emotional mess. She wanted to change into something elegant, something sophisticated, but at the same time she was feeling so vulnerable inside she just knew that she did not stand a chance of carrying it off should Vere raise a querying eyebrow as if to assert, I'm honoured—all this so I can rebuke you over...

In the end she left her hair loose, the way it was, and went down the stairs in the smart but—in her view—quite ordinary dress she had worn at dinner.

'Everything all right?' Vere queried, rising to his feet as she entered the drawing-room.

With her? No. With the children? 'Fine,' she answered.

'Take a seat,' he invited, pointing to a nearby comfortable-looking chair. And as she complied, 'Would you like something to drink?' he enquired civilly.

So far, so good. It was not to be any quick 'so take that' interview, then? Fabienne began to relax. 'A gin and tonic would be nice.' Grief! Listen to her! Her heart was racing like an express train, yet she sounded formal, precise—when what she wanted to do was to fling herself into his arms and beg him to love her.

Vere came back from the drinks table with a gin and tonic for her and a Scotch and water for himself. Placing both on a low table next to her, he moved a chair close up to the other side of the table and lowered his long length into it.

Fabienne looked at him—and away again. There seemed less than a yard separating them, and she had never been more aware of him. Needing something to do, she stretched out a hand to her drink and picked it up and took a sip, wondering why, when Vere looked so perfectly relaxed, she was suddenly feeling uptight again.

'Any problems with Kitty and John today?' Vere wanted to know.

'Kitty—more than John, I think—is missing her mother a little. Nothing serious,' Fabienne hastened to add, 'but just a quite natural reaction I believe, with or without their special circumstances.'

For some quite long moments Vere stared at her, his look holding hers, refusing to let her look away. Then, 'You're good with them, understanding,' he murmured, and Fabienne felt relaxed and tense all at the same time.

'They're no trouble,' she replied a degree huskily, feeling herself start to unwind that it did not after all look as though Vere had asked to see her to remonstrate with her over some matter, but seemed more—in the absence of a parent—to want to enquire into the twins' welfare that day. At the same time, though, Fabienne could not help but feel on edge. Her love for him was at the root of that, she knew. He was so close, so wonderful, so—so everything, and she was terrified of giving herself away. 'Alex, my brother,' she suddenly blurted out from nowhere, 'he called today.'

Immediately, she wished she had not said that. But it was too late now. 'Did you not see him yesterday?' Vere asked, and Fabienne just could not tell him that Alex had called more to see Rachel than her.

'Mmm, I did.' She nodded. 'But we're close—and—er—he had business this way,' she invented, in the interests of saving Vere from hurt if his sharp brain saw beyond what she was saying. To her utmost relief, he appeared to take what she had just said at face value. Though, to her surprise, asked after another male of her acquaintance.

'See anything of Lyndon Davies today?'

His tone had been casual but, recalling the spat they'd had the last time Lyndon's name had come up, Fabienne took another sip of her drink before replying. 'Rachel delivered Kitty and John to school this morning, but I saw Lyndon this afternoon when he was collecting his niece, Sadie.' Curiosity suddenly got the better of her. 'Any problem with that?'

Vere gave her a steady look but, while she would have loved it had he owned to being the teeniest bit jealous—what a hope; she must be going mental—Fabienne knew in her heart that it was more that Vere must be forever aware of who, in the interests of the children's safety, she was getting friendly with locally.

Her question, however, went unanswered. Though, albeit indirectly, Lyndon was still in there somewhere when, his tone less affable than it had been, 'You took a long time to eat your dinner last night.'

Had it been that she had just gone out for dinner she might have agreed with him. 'We went on to a jazz concert.' She saw no reason not to tell him.

'I didn't know you liked jazz!'

Fabienne did not like at all the harsh note that was creeping into his tone. 'I expect that there are a lot of things I like which you know nothing about!' she returned sharply—and hated that, when things had seemed to be going so well, it looked as though they would start fighting at any moment.

'Then perhaps——' he began—and seemed to hesitate.

But if he was, for once, pausing to choose his words before he verbally floored her, Fabienne was not of a mind to wait around while he did so. 'If you don't mind, I'll get off to bed,' she selected as an exit line, lest he thought it bothered her one bit that they had ended up rowing yet again. She placed her glass down on the table and stood up. Then found that Vere was on his feet, too, and that she still needed an exit line. 'If Rachel should ring——' she began, off the top of her head—and was straight away floored anyway.

'She's already phoned!' Vere stated crisply.

Fabienne flicked her glance from him so he should not see the hurt in her eyes, the hurt and pain of jealousy. 'Goodnight!' she bade him off-handedly and, not waiting for his reply, she went quickly.

No doubt if Rachel had not telephoned him he would have telephoned Rachel. When had she phoned? After dinner, obviously, so as not to upset the children if they were missing her. Was it just to enquire after her children that she had phoned? Or had she rung because she had wanted to hear Vere's voice? And what about Vere—had he wanted to hear Rachel's voice, too? Was he missing her like crazy? And—what about Alex?

Fabienne got into bed wishing with all she had that she had never gone down the stairs. Life was hell, love was hell, and she wanted ... she wanted ... Oh, dammit, she wanted that which she could not have.

She eventually fell into a light, troubled sleep but awakened at twenty-past one to see that her door was open and to be able to make out, in the glow from the one landing light left on, that Kitty had come into her room and was standing by her bed.

In an instant Fabienne was wide awake, but she kept her voice calm and gentle so as not to startle the child if she was sleep-walking. 'Hello, love,' she murmured, and discovered that Kitty was not sleep-walking but fretting for her mother.

'I'm not sleepy,' Kitty told her unhappily.

Fabienne wondered what her own mother would do in such circumstances. It took only a moment to find an answer. 'Climb in,' she invited, and Kitty needed no more bidding than that.

Inside ten minutes Kitty was sound asleep—and Fabienne was still wide awake. Half an hour after that and Fabienne, listening to Kitty's steady rhythmic breathing, formed the opinion that the child was so solidly asleep she would not waken for hours—not even in the unlikely event of the house falling down.

Carefully Fabienne slid out of bed, and carefully set about picking up the lightweight child. Her task of carrying Kitty back to her own bed was made easier by the fact that Kitty had left the door open when she had entered. Fabienne's difficulty arose, however, when, on padding quietly along to Kitty's room, she discovered that Kitty had carefully closed her own door behind her.

Fabienne was in the throes of adjusting her hold on the child in order to have a hand free to open the door when suddenly, and with a furiously racing heart, she realised that she had no need to bother. Help was at hand!

She had thought she had made not a sound, but she must have done, for someone else was awake too! Vere's hand got to the doorknob first as, taking in the situation in one glance, he opened the door to Kitty's room and led the way in.

Fabienne was by then feeling just so much nonsense. It was so unexpected; he was so dear, so tall—even with bare feet seeming taller than ever—in a robe that ended near his knees and showed a pair of long and handsome, if hairy, totally masculine legs.

Vere it was who opened up the child's bed and then turned to take Kitty from her. And Vere it was who gently laid the sleeping child down. Fabienne covered her over and stood and looked at her for a few moments to make sure she would sleep on—and then silently, with Vere right there beside her, she tiptoed from the room.

It was Vere who, without making a sound, closed Kitty's door. Fabienne, now suddenly conscious that the neckline of her thin cotton nightdress was more décolleté than décolleté and that from Vere's lofty height he must have a fine view of a goodly portion of her shapely breasts, walked on.

She halted when she reached her door and thought Vere would go walking on to his room. But he did not, but halted too. And all at once Fabienne did not want to remember that they had parted on unfriendly terms, and did not want him to remember it either—so searched desperately for something light and friendly to say in parting.

'We can't go on meeting like this,' she joked, and found she was staring straight into a pair of direct grey eyes. Eyes that roved her face, eyes that took in every feature, eyes that whispered over her scant covering, eyes that lingered for a moment where her breasts pushed at what material they could find to cover them. Eyes that came back to her eyes and just looked at her. 'K-Kitty couldn't sleep,' Fabienne added in a rush.

'Neither can I,' Vere drawled, and there was no animosity in his voice, only humour, and she loved him.

'She's only seven,' Fabienne replied, conscious of the way his glance moved to the corners of her upward-turning mouth.

'I wish—I wish I were seven,' he murmured, his eyes dancing—and Fabienne burst out laughing.

'If you think you're coming into my bed——' she began—and then, all of a sudden, she was not laughing any more because the look on Vere's face was all at once serious. 'Vere...' she choked—and that was it.

The choked sound of his name on her lips was all it took for him to reach slowly for her. To gather her into his arms. Whether he saw encouragement in the fact that she had called out his first name she neither knew nor cared. He was warm. She wanted his warmth. She felt she had been out in the cold for too long. Willingly, she went into his arms.

For long, silent moments he looked down at her and then, as a shuddery kind of sigh escaped him, so his head came down—and a world of new emotions awakened in Fabienne.

A breath of a sigh escaped her, too, as their lips met, met and caressed, met and kissed—and kissed again. They were still in each other's arms when Vere moved with her into her room and closed the door.

Warmed by him, held close to his heart, his strong arms around her, Fabienne reached up and wound her arms around him. Words were unnecessary and their mouths met again, Vere lighting a fire in her that flamed into a roar of raw emotion.

He broke his kiss and stared down at her in the light of the night. She wished she could read his expression but there was not sufficient light for that. And did it matter?

She stretched up and kissed him and, wanting to be closer still, she pressed against him, delighting in the groan that left him. Then experienced more flames of fire when she felt his hands move down to her hips and, through the thin material of her cotton covering, felt his hands burn into her as he pressed her yet closer to him.

'Oh, Vere,' she cried on a strangled sound, and arched back her throat as his passion soared and he traced more burning kisses down the sides of her face, her eyes, her arched throat, her breasts.

She wanted him; desperately did she want him. She knew that as his hands caressed, upwards now, until the globes of her thrusting breasts were captured in his hold.

She wanted to cry his name again, but could not. She pressed against him, and kissed him, and loved him, adored him and wanted to be his. Their kiss broke, and she laid her head against his chest, discovered that his robe had parted and knew more ecstasy at being allowed the freedom to kiss his bare chest.

She felt his shiver of delight, and the next thing she knew his hands were caressing her body, were raising her nightdress, gently, unhurriedly, giving her as much time as she wanted should she wish to object.

But she did not wish to object, but clutched at him for only the briefest of moments as a strand of shyness came out of nowhere. Then she kissed him, and stood a little away, so he could take her nightdress over her head.

She had never stood naked before a man, but it seemed natural somehow that she should, without embarrassment or shame, stand before Vere then, and feel only a modicum of shyness when in what light there was he gazed at the perfect outline of her body.

'Oh, my darling, my brave darling,' broke from him as his gaze left the tips of her breasts and he gently gathered her into his arms.

A shuddering sigh shook her and Vere removed his robe and pulled her up against him. Fabienne swallowed on a knot of panic, a knot of not knowing where she was, a knot of wanting him but of being in a world where theory was about to become practice. She knew all about the facts of life but knew nothing of loving, of having an all-vibrant, throbbing male standing this close, like a second skin. She thought she might faint.

'Vere!' she gasped chokily, and clutched on to him.

'Don't be alarmed,' he breathed, and cradled her gently—as though he knew, he really knew, what she was feeling.

She almost told him then how much she truly loved him but, as though more intent on dealing with any fear she might have, Vere took a step away.

'Vere!' She called his name in sudden panic that, having brought her to this pitch, he might leave her.

'It's all right,' he soothed, and stayed, his arm around her naked shoulder as he guided her over to the bed.

She smiled. He could not see, but she smiled, and they turned to each other and clung and kissed, and Vere held her by her upper arms while gently, and again unhurriedly, he traced kisses over her face and eyes, over her throat and naked shoulders and kissed his way to her breasts where he kissed each one in turn, and built in her an absolute frenzy of delight when his mouth captured the hardened pink tips he had created and she felt the moist insides of his mouth as he moulded each pink tip and swollen globe in turn—caressing that peak with his tongue, nibbling her.

She was almost swooning with rapture and a low moan escaped her when Vere's mouth left her breasts and he kissed his way down to her navel, her belly, and her thighs.

'Vere!' she choked, and suddenly he had picked her up and she felt the wonder of him, his broad manly chest, as he raised her and then gently laid her down on the bed.

In a second he had joined her on the bed, his naked body stretched out down the length of her own, and she knew that, soon, he would make her his.

'C-can I touch you?' she asked nervously.

'Oh, sweet love,' he breathed joyously, and Fabienne kissed him and stroked his hair-roughened chest before she put her arms around him and, with his body half over hers, her hands travelled down his back.

She had her hands on his unclothed hips when her need for him spiralled out of all bounds, so she pressed nearer, heard him groan, and moved so that his body was almost entirely over hers, Vere in turn pressing her down, down, down into the mattress.

Fabienne was in a mindless vortex of wanting—her body, her thighs having a will of their own as she prepared to welcome him, to hold him.

She wanted ease from this fierce need, had to have the comfort of him. Wanted comfort from him as she would comfort him. Comfort—comfort! Suddenly that word would not go out of her head. Suddenly that word comfort refused to budge. And suddenly that word was screaming, shrieking through her brain. She tried to eject it; it was coming between her and the love she wanted with Vere. It was... Comfort!

In substitution for Rachel she had, by inviting Kitty to sleep in her bed, comforted the child. Comfort. Substitute for Rachel! Her bed. Vere kissed her. Tenderly he parted her thighs, tenderly his sensitive fingers caressed her thighs. But—it wasn't right. Suddenly—comfort, substitute—no *way* was it right!

And, '*No*!' she cried in sudden horror—and, as though electrified, she in one movement pushed, pulled, jerked and rolled, until she was clear of him.

'No?' His tone was incredulous. A second ago she had been his for the taking!

'No!' she repeated while she still had the strength.

'But—my dear——'

'No!' she gasped.

'Don't be afraid——'

'*No*!' she cried in panic, fear that he would not take no for an answer adding to that panic.

'But——'

She had her back to him and was glad for, treacherous body, she still wanted him with a need that was crucifying. 'For God's sake—you're not a man to beg, are you?' she cried, terrified that her body, her heart, might yet ignore the truth that her head was insisting on telling her.

But it seemed that she was not the only one with an outsized pride for, after what seemed an agony of silence, his voice came again, curt and clipped this time as he proved that he begged from no one by telling her cuttingly, 'I assure you, my dear, that if there's any begging to be done around here for——' He paused, and then added deliberately, insultingly '—sexual favours, you'll be the one down on your knees.'

With that he rose from the bed and left—and Fabienne again knew how interminably long a night could be when one's heart was aching.

By dawn she had been over everything that had led up to Vere taking her in his arms, and what had followed, countless times. Once she was weak enough to wonder if perhaps it had been merely nerves attacking, after all, that had seen her call a halt to Vere's lovemaking. While she admitted to feeling a snatch shy here

and there, she had not thought she had been nervous.
But had she been?

That weakening thought passed and, almost immediately and with renewed vigour, she was back to knowing
that the reason why Vere had not been able to sleep, why
he had been still awake when she had carried Kitty back
to her bed, was that he had Rachel too much on his
mind. Thoughts of Rachel had kept him awake.

Had he been thinking of Rachel when he had called
out, 'Oh, my darling, my brave darling'? Had Rachel
been in his mind with that 'Oh, sweet love'? When previously she had been oblivious to embarrassment,
Fabienne was suddenly cringing with it as such thoughts
racked her.

By dawn she had been through everything yet again
and again and felt utterly and completely drained, pride
her only salvation. It was that pride, which said she
would be a substitute for no one where Vere was concerned, that decided matters for her. A mammoth pride
decreed that, as soon as Rachel returned tomorrow, she
must leave. Rachel was so much better than she had
been—the mere fact that she was again driving and had
decided to make things up with her parents was proof
enough of that.

Fabienne was heartily glad when the time came around
for her to attend to Kitty and John. She had been
showered and dressed for ages—and was relieved to have
something to do.

For herself she would have missed breakfast—and
every other meal—rather than have to sit facing Vere.
But, for the moment, the children and their mental and
physical welfare was still all-important.

'Are we ready?' she smiled to them as they were about
to go down the stairs.

A few minutes later, with the children in front, Fabienne entered the breakfast-room. Vere was there—and her ridiculous heart *still* turned somersaults! She was saved having to speak to him when the twins at once engaged him in conversation. Not that he noticed the lack of her usual 'Good morning' for he did not so much as glance her way.

She wished that she could get angry about that—ye gods, they'd been *naked* with each other last night!—but she could not get angry. She felt beaten, whipped, and all she wanted was that he would hurry up with his breakfast and go.

But, when the time came when he usually made a move to go to his office, that morning, strangely, he did not. In fact, he was still sitting there talking to Kitty and John when the time came for them to go and see Mrs Hobbs about their lunchboxes.

Since she had absolutely no intention of being left alone with him, Fabienne left it to the very last moment to interrupt and tell the twins, 'We'd better go and see Mrs Hobbs or we're going to be late.'

Oh, how she wished that she had been able to keep her eyes off Vere. But she could not, and she glanced his way—and found he was looking directly at her. There was no smile on his face for her, nor even a hint of one. His look was steady, but stern. Solemn and somehow—waiting?

She dismissed that notion as nonsense. What would he be waiting for, for goodness' sake? Fabienne wrenched her gaze from him, glad that no one could hear the thunder in her heart and, still without a word to him, she shepherded the children kitchenwards.

Vere was on her mind the whole time she chatted and drove the children to school. He obviously had a late appointment that morning and had no need to go to work at his usual time.

She kept an eye open for his car passing—which it would have to—the whole while she was at the school gates, but saw not a sign of it.

With the happenings of the night so much to the forefront of her mind, Fabienne felt disinclined to hurry back to Brackendale where she stood the risk—if he had not left yet—of meeting Vere in the hall.

'There's another jazz concert next month.' Lyndon Davies came over to see her when he had seen his niece safely into the school playground. And Fabienne put off her return to Brackendale by staying to chat to him for a good half-hour—and in all that time not one car of the make of Vere's passed that way.

By the time she was in her own car and driving back to the house, Fabienne's intelligence had been working overtime. She had by then relegated the idea that Vere had a late appointment to the bin. He was just not the type of man who, because of a late appointment, would delay going to his office by more than an hour. He was the type of man who would have other work to keep him busy the whole while.

Which left there having to be another reason for his delayed departure—or, for that matter, a reason why he was not going in to work at all. And she knew exactly what that reason was.

Fabienne left her car at the front of the house—it would be easier for when she carried her belongings out. For, by then, she knew that by no stretch of the imagination would she be waiting until tomorrow for Rachel's return before she left. By then she had well and truly got the message.

By then it had become exceptionally clear to her that Vere was bitterly regretting what had taken place be-

tween them in the small hours—and now wanted her to
leave. It was manifestly obvious. Oh, how foolish she
had been to believe that to leave had been her
prerogative!

By not going to work that morning Vere was clearly
stating that he would stay home to be on call should the
children need him. And just as clearly, he was stating
that her services were no longer required.

Fabienne entered by the front door of the proud
opinion then that nobody told her 'on your way'. She
would go straight up and pack. In a half-hour she could
be out of here. She would have to stop off at the school
to give some light and plausible explanation for why she
would not be there after school, that was important, but
in a half-hour...

There was no sign of Vere, though, as she went towards the stairs, and then she hesitated, her heart lifting.
Had she got it wrong? Did Vere, who knew the area far
better than her, know of a different route to London
that did not involve passing by the school gates?

Her nerves started to bite when she found she could
no more go on up those stairs than fly—not until she
knew for sure.

She did an about-turn and, with her heart tripping an
agitated rhythm, she went to where she felt certain he
would be if he was at home. Outside the study door she
hesitated, then found she had to swallow hard before she
knocked.

And, having knocked, she swallowed again and hoped
with all she had that her knock would not be answered
and that Vere had gone to his office. But a sound from
within told her that she had been right the first time,
that Vere was home—and that she was redundant.

Her spirits were at basement level when the door
opened and a cool, steady-eyed Vere stood there. He

waited for her to speak—and she had nothing to say. Worse, as treacherous thoughts of their nakedness with each other last night came and tripped her up, she went scarlet. But, much worse than that, as his eyes stayed on her face and he witnessed her crimson colour, she wanted to die.

Which was why she was never more glad to find that she still had some backbone, for suddenly she knew that before he gave her notice to leave his employ she was going to get in first to give him notice, to tell him she did not want the job anyway.

With all that stewing away inside her, not to mention the fact that Vere's eyes were still scrutinising her face and taking in every detail, it amazed her that her voice, when she spoke, came out sounding very cool and controlled as she enquired, 'May I see you?'

Her coolness was not lost on him, she could tell that from the way his eyes narrowed. But he nodded his agreement, and his voice was not only cool but arrogant too, as he replied, 'It will save me coming to see you.'

And from that Fabienne at once knew that there was no doubt that he was about to terminate her employment. All she could hope, as she battled with nerves and butterflies, was that she managed to get out of Brackendale with at least some dignity.

CHAPTER NINE

ODDLY, however, Vere did not invite her into his study but, to confuse her more than somewhat, he came out without a word and led the way to the drawing-room.

But she did not like at all the feeling that, like some puppy, she was having to follow at his heels. So that by the time they were in the drawing-room she had banished confusion and become determined to get her words in first.

He turned to close the drawing-room door as she followed him in but, as she opened her mouth, to her astonishment he rapped, 'You took your time getting back here!'

Her jaw dropped—my heavens, he couldn't wait to be rid of her! 'I didn't know I had to clock in!' she flew. She might feel floored but, by thunder, he was never going to know it. She saw the glint of steel in his eyes at her spirited response and lost no more time in tacking on angrily, 'I want to leave!' There, she fumed, pick the bones out of that! And wanted to hit him when that was precisely what he did.

'Why?'

The question was blunt. 'Why?' she echoed. Good grief, it had been a toss-up which one of them got the notice to leave in first!

'You're upset because of what took place between us last night?' he questioned forthrightly—and again Fabienne wanted to hit him. *That* had nothing to do with it! Well, perhaps it did. It was all part and parcel of it anyhow. But trust him not to flinch from bringing *that* up.

'There's no need to go into that!' she replied tartly. 'Just——'

'There's every need to go into it!' he cut her off grimly. 'Last night you——'

Oh, God, she couldn't take this. 'Last night I came on to you in a big way—is that what you're going to accuse me of?' she flared hostilely. 'Are you going to tell me that it was all my fault—that you, that you...?' Her voice faltered—and broke.

Swiftly she turned her back on him. No way was he going to see her in tears. She half turned, wishing she had made for the door, but Vere seemed to be guarding the door. She moved further away and went to stand by one of the long windows in the room.

She looked out, but saw nothing. However, she thought she had regained her self-control and would not break down in floods of pent-up tears. Then she heard a sound close by, and suddenly a thrill of electricity was shooting through her because Vere had come over to the window, too, and had placed an arm about her shoulders! Then he turned her to face him!

She kept her head bent, certain she would not look at him. Yet the compulsion to do so proved so strong and she just had to look up. And her heart turned over because, as Vere looked down at her, she could see no sign of harshness in him. All sign of sternness had gone and, while his expression was still serious, his voice was kinder than it had been when he answered, 'Last night you were warm and wonderful in my arms, and if anyone came on to anyone, it was me to you.'

She wanted to swallow, but would not. His voice, his kindness, was making a nonsense of her—which made her chances of getting out of there with her dignity intact about nil. 'Yes, well, that's beside the point!' she retaliated with as much frost as she could muster.

'Is it?' Direct grey eyes were boring into hers, refusing to let her look away—oh, help her, somebody!

'You ... I ...' she tried helplessly, but knew she stood no chance—not while he still had his arm about her shoulders.

Yet she did not seem to have the will to tell him to take it away. That was until with blinding clarity she recalled the way she had seen him with his arm around his stepsister-in-law, and at once jealousy and pain were her master.

She stiffened in his hold, and through clenched teeth ordered in no uncertain fashion, 'Take your arm from me!' And, when he was not quick enough to comply, Fabienne stepped angrily out of his hold, her fury taking her control as she cried, 'I refuse to be used as a substitute for——' She gasped in horror at what she had just said. She wanted it unsaid. So badly did she want it unsaid, ignored, forgotten. But, as she had known, Vere was not a man who hid from anything.

He stilled. 'Substitute?' he queried quietly—and she knew, just knew, that he would not leave it alone until she had explained what she meant.

She threw him an angry look. He knew, damn him, without her having to explain. 'Don't pretend with me!' she tossed at him accusingly.

'What have I——?'

'You know...'

'Fabienne, I——'

She did not want him using her first name; to hear her name on his lips weakened her. 'Oh, for goodness' sake!' she erupted and, having given in her notice, 'I'm off!' she snapped without ceremony, and stormed to the door.

As fast as she went, though—and she did not hang about—Vere was at the door before her. 'No!' he snarled, and it was all she could do not to kick his shins.

'Let me out of here!' she spat.

'Not until you've controlled that spirited temper of yours and explained——'

'*Me* explain!' she spluttered—the cheek of it!

'You think I've some explaining to do?'

'I... You...' Oh, lord, he was tying her up in knots!

She glared at him angrily—and saw some of the chill in his eyes thaw. 'Look, I know you're upset, and I understand that,' he stated evenly. 'But if you'd try to calm down and——'

'Why should I calm down?'

'Hell's teeth, I knew from the first that I was going to have trouble with you!' he ground out. Then took a controlling deep breath and with a firm hold on her elbow insisted on leading her back into the room. 'Why not sit down and——?'

'I don't want to sit down,' she butted in, pulling her arm out of his hold and receiving one of his 'my God, I'll sort you in a minute' looks, though manfully he hung on to his control. 'Why should I sit down?'

'Because I should like you to,' he answered tautly.

'Why can't I just—leave?'

'Because you owe me an explanation for why you want to leave,' he pointed out—which, at any other time, she might have thought perfectly reasonable.

But this wasn't any other time. Last night she had been in his arms, last night had been wonderful and loving—only he didn't love her and, in fact, had only been using her as a substitute love.

'I don't——' she began, as jealousy and pain started to sting again. But then it all at once occurred to her that if Vere was about to dismiss her then he was going a funny way about it. She shot him a startled look and, the thought in her head, out it came. 'I thought you were going to ask me to leave?' she said slowly.

'Why the hell would I want to do that?' he asked, and seemed so genuinely surprised by the notion that Fabienne could only stare at him.

'You—you said I'd saved you from coming to see me,' she murmured falteringly.

'So I did, but not because I wanted you to go.'

'Oh!' she exclaimed, and desperately tried to get her head together, but nothing was making very much sense just then. 'You wanted to—er—ask me to—um—forget all about l-last night?' she guessed, while with part of her brain she wondered what she was doing still standing there if to retain her dignity was so all-important.

Vere opened his mouth as though he would answer her question. But then must have changed his mind. 'Look, we need to talk,' he stated flatly, and Fabienne realised that, since it did not seem as if he intended to dispense with her services, to a man of his principles it would seem only right and natural that, following on from what had taken place between them last night, he would want it all out in the open before he then went on to request that she forget all about it, and to assure her that it would not happen again. 'Would you sit down?' he requested.

She could not think that it would take him all that long to say what he clearly felt had to be said before they went back to the status quo. Nor, since she still had every intention of insisting on leaving—which would negate his having to tell her anything—could she think of any reason why she should take a seat.

Which left it down to her treacherous heart, and her love for him, and her deep, subconscious need to stay with him for just a short while longer before she severed all ties, to make her go over to a nearby couch and sit down.

She waited only until Vere was seated in the chair nearby and it was an innate honesty that caused her to tell him, 'Regardless of anything you say, I'm still leaving.'

For long moments, his expression inscrutable, Vere looked at her. And, if that was not unnerving enough, when he opened his mouth and commented softly, 'Oh, I do hope not, my dear,' Fabienne was again a jumbled mass of emotions.

'Well, I——' she began, trying for a firm note, but the choked sound that came out caused her to break off. She swallowed—had to—did not miss the alert look that came to Vere's eyes and knew that she had to dispel at once any notion he might have gleaned that just a simple endearment from him could throw her emotionally out of gear. 'Well, I am not,' she began again, heartily glad to hear that her voice was firmer, 'not,' she repeated, 'going to be made use of by anybody.'

Vere was silent as he studied her mutinous expression. But he was just as smart as she had thought him and had soon sifted through her answer, and was again not going to have anything hiding in dark corners. 'By that "anybody" I assume you mean me.' She did not deny it. Why should she? But his clever brain was at work again and, to her horror, Fabienne found that he had delved into that which she would by far rather he had not delved and matched it to what she had just said when, with his eyes fixed on hers, he quietly brought out, 'You stated a few minutes ago that you refused to be used as a substitute.' The directness of his look refused to allow her to look away. 'So tell me about it.'

Fabienne stared obstinately back at him. She'd be damned if she'd tell him anything! He knew anyway.

But as she looked mulishly at him, so Vere sat patiently—waiting. She flicked a glance to the door to judge the distance if she made a run for it. Vere followed her glance—and she knew that she would never make it. And still he waited.

He couldn't keep her there by force, she fumed, at the same time wondering at that treacherous part of her that she had never known existed until she had fallen in love—that treacherous part of her that, when the old Fabienne would have charged out of there with her nose in the air anyway, seemed to be compelling her to stay, to hear this out to the end. As if somehow she and her treacherous heart wanted to hear Vere make his 'it will never happen again' apology!

And still he waited. And that was when, throwing him an exasperated look, Fabienne started to get really mad with herself—and him—and because of that anger became unwary!

'I refuse to be used as a substitute for the woman you love!' she exploded, wished that she had not—but even while she wanted those unintentionally spoken words back she was ready to hurl more at him. Though she was taken out of her stride by the look of sheer surprise on Vere's face.

He coped with his surprise, though. But even as he replied, 'I assure you I should never do that,' his eyes were still watchful on her.

'Thanks!' she snapped tartly, which was ridiculous she owned, because a moment ago she had been furious and unhappy that he had last night used her as a substitute—yet now she did not like it either that he had stated he would never use her as a substitute for his love. 'You weren't so very fussy last night!' she hurled at him—and inwardly groaned that her tongue was running away from her.

But there was a look in Vere's eyes that told her he was more alert than ever and that, a few more hasty, angry, unthought-out barbs from her and, if she was not careful, it would not take him long to realise that she was heart and soul in love with him.

'I hope,' he began severely, never for a moment taking his eyes from her face, 'that you're not suggesting I could think of any other woman while I held you in my arms last night.'

Her stomach was churning, her heart fluttering, even the palms of her hands felt moist as she weathered Vere's severe look that seemed so sincere. She felt she was drowning—which left her with not a lot to reply save what she hoped was a scornful-sounding, 'Huh!'

Something in his expression quickened. 'You're jealous?'

'You're joking!' she derided.

He took that on the chin, though Fabienne was certain that he did not give two hoots whether she was jealous or not. 'I've hurt your pride in some way?' Vere questioned, plainly having done a rethink.

Fabienne had a rethink, too, a very fast one, and found she could live with him knowing that he had hurt her pride rather than that he should know her love for him had caused her to be deep green with jealousy.

'What do you expect?' she challenged. 'I'm not used to men making love to me while they've some other female on their mind.'

'Good God!' he bellowed. 'You seriously believe that?' Fabienne had to own that she felt a little shaken by his vehemence, and then found that he was too angry with her to wait for an answer. 'Leaving aside the fact that you aren't used to men making love to you at all to the extent of our involvement with each other last night,' he said shortly, 'who the hell did you think I had on my mind when we were making love?'

Again Fabienne wanted to run from the room. And yet there was something about Vere, the attitude he was taking, that made her want to stay. Had she got it wrong? Had jealousy clouded her vision?

'I...' She swallowed hard, and somehow then—urgently—she needed to know from this man whom she had believed would hide from nothing—the truth. 'I thought you c-cared for Rachel.' She pushed the words out from between her teeth—and had her heart sink down to her boots at his reply.

'Well, naturally I care for her,' he stated without hesitation, and Fabienne started to feel quite miserable. 'She's my stepbrother's widow and has had one hell of a time,' Vere continued, then abruptly stopped. If he had seemed surprised before then the look he now threw her was one of complete and utter amazement. And, 'Confound it!' he muttered, as if still not crediting what his intelligence had brought him. 'You—didn't think I was in *love* with Rachel, did you?'

'Why shouldn't I think it? Only on Monday I saw you with your arm around her, comforting her!' she flared and, as the pain of that memory started to nip, 'What the hell did you expect me to do when—rather late in the day, I'll admit—it suddenly dawned on me that I was merely the substitute?'

'My G——' He broke off, clearly shattered. 'So *that's* why you—late in the day an understatement—told me "no!".'

'I hope I'm allowed my pride,' she retorted stiffly, and got to her feet. Now seemed as good a time as any to leave.

But Vere, it seemed, had other ideas, and he was on his feet too, and had taken the few paces necessary to

enable him to stand in front of her. 'Oh, no, my dear,'
he said, looking down into her wide and wary large
brown eyes. 'Not yet.'

Fabienne was worried by that 'not yet', and weakened
by that 'my dear', and as her knees suddenly turned to
water it seemed a good idea—with Vere this close—to
sit back down again. 'You'll let me know when, I trust?'
she asked, glad to feel the couch beneath her once more.

'As uppity as ever—even though you're as nervous as
I am!' Vere replied, to her astonishment and, as it sank
in that not only had he seen her nervousness but *he* was
nervous too, went on, 'You'll know when.' And to her
alarm, instead of returning to the chair he had vacated,
he chose to take the seat next to her on the couch. It
was then that he turned to look at her and, close again,
there was no way Fabienne could avoid looking at him.
'*If*,' he said with emphasis, 'you still want to go when
you've heard me out, so be it. But first I want you to
hear me out.'

Oh, Vere. She loved him. What could she do? 'I hope
this won't take long,' she answered sharply. 'In the children's interest, I think it would be better if I'm gone
before they return from school.'

'Did anyone ever tell you that you are the most mad-
dening bloody woman ever to——?'

'It's no good you trying to sweet-talk me into staying!'
she rallied—and Vere suddenly burst out laughing.

'My God, what am I going to do with you? You're
driving me nuts!'

That sobered her. She liked the sound of it—even if
she knew full well that she could not trust it. 'What did
I do?' she questioned, and could have died that her voice
had gone all husky again.

'Give me a year and I'll tell you,' he answered, his
laughter gone, his look unfaltering. 'Though to get one

matter out of the way, you have it completely wrong if you think that I'm in love with Rachel.'

'Oh!' she exclaimed, her heart starting to leap in all directions. 'But you do care for her?'

'I do. She's my stepbrother's widow, the mother of his children—and she's been to hell and back. Anything I could do for her to make her path easier than it has been, I would.' He paused and, looking steadily at her, he went on, 'She's had a foul time trying to shake off her depression but now, at last, there's every sign that she's coming out of it.'

'Oh, she's much better now than she was,' Fabienne heartily agreed.

'Thanks to you,' Vere commented and added softly, 'and your brother.'

Her eyes widened. 'You know about that?' she gasped.

'I know that Rachel's in a panic because she thinks she's falling in love again,' he confided.

Fabienne stared at him, her brain, her heart racing. Vere did not seem in any way upset to know that Rachel might be falling in love with Alex.

'I—think Alex feels pretty much the same about Rachel,' she said slowly. 'He—um—called yesterday hoping to see her, but she'd already left.' She took a shaky breath and, because she could not believe she had got it so wrong, she just had to ask, 'D-did Rachel tell you how she—um—feels?'

'She was in a panic, as I mentioned, and buttonholed me the moment I arrived home on Monday. As you must know, she and Alex dined *à deux* on Saturday. Rachel didn't say what they'd discussed, and I didn't ask, but since then she's been mixed up and in a flap emotionally—and of the opinion that she needed some space to think. Only Alex phoned her on Monday—and while that pleased her, afterwards she started to go to pieces.'

'Oh, poor Rachel. I wish she'd said something. I might have been able to...'

'She wanted to confide in you. But not only are you Alex's sister, you'd told her that you liked his ex-wife.'

'I like Rachel, too!'

'I know that. How else could you have acted so warmly sensitive to her depression?' he smiled, and Fabienne's heart turned over.

'I hope I'd be sensitive with anyone suffering depression,' she mumbled.

'I don't doubt it, my dear,' he murmured, and her bones turned to so much jelly. 'But,' he went on as if wanting this out of the way, 'Rachel was in such a stew when she rushed to meet me on Monday that it was instinctive to put a——' He broke off, and then stated deliberately, 'A comforting and stepbrotherly arm about her.'

'Oh!' Fabienne choked, as everything about Monday fell into place. By placing a comforting arm about Rachel's shoulder, Vere had been doing nothing more than Alex, her brother, would if she was upset.

'Oh, indeed,' Vere took up, and asked, 'You do see now that I was merely sympathising, encouraging in the best way a mere male can think to do in such circumstances?'

'Yes, of course,' Fabienne smiled. And, aware that she would be kissing his feet at any moment if she did not watch it, she thought—the excuse of wounded pride having been honourably resolved—that it might be an idea if she went elsewhere and found herself something useful to do. 'And I'm sure that if both Rachel and Alex can learn to trust again they'll look after each other. Alex is a very honourable man,' she told Vere, and then grew afraid that she was, in her anxiety to be elsewhere, just rattling on as she sought for a neat exit line. 'He would never hurt her.' She found she could not stop gabbling on as still she searched. 'I was so afraid that you might be hurt——' Aghast, she came to an abrupt halt. Alarm bells shrieked out warnings. Had she just said what she thought she'd said?

Apparently she had, for a darted glance to Vere's face showed he was looking a tinge stunned—and delighted! She jerkily made to get to her feet. But, quicker than she, Vere caught a swift hold of her hands and held her down on the couch beside him.

'Why the rush?' He smiled with poleaxing charm. 'This is just getting interesting.' Stubbornly, her insides churning over, she stayed mute—and had to suffer Vere studying her mulish expression for some long seconds. Then, his voice soft, unhurried, 'You've been afraid—for me?' he questioned quietly.

'You know how it is—all for the underdog.' She made a brave stab at getting on top of the quite dreadful situation she had put herself in.

'Underdog?' he echoed, a man who had never been—nor, she suspected, ever would be—an underdog. 'Because you thought I was in love with Rachel, but that your brother might win her?'

She hated him and his sharp logical mind, not to mention that she was dying a thousand deaths where she sat. 'It seemed likely,' she replied stiffly, and wished he would let go her hands because just the feel of his skin, his warmth, was making a nonsense of any brainpower.

But then Vere said something that was so startling, so shattering that, while her eyes went saucer-wide in disbelief, she was glad to have something to clutch on to. For, looking down into her agitated eyes, he paused, seemed to hesitate but for a moment longer and then, a kind of strain starting to show on his face, 'How could I be in love with Rachel, my dear,' he asked, 'when it is you who hold my whole heart?'

A gasp escaped her, her eyes shot wide, and she clung quite desperately on to his hands. 'I don't!' she argued with what voice she could find.

'Oh, but you do,' he replied firmly. 'As you have almost from the beginning—only I've been too blind until so very recently to see.'

She swallowed hard, and had no thought in her head that he might witness it—and have confirmation that 'nervous' was a misnomer for what she felt. 'H-how?' she questioned, with no intention then of going an inch from the room until he had answered—until she knew more. For it could not be so, could it? Oh, dear heaven, could it?

'How defeats me,' Vere confessed, his eyes never leaving her face. 'All I can tell you is that from the moment I saw you my world has been turned upside-down.'

Amazed, she stared at him, and again all she could answer was a choky, 'H-how?'

He smiled, whether to encourage her or because of the encouragement she was giving him by staying to ask questions she was too het-up just then to decide. But smile he did, his look gentle on her still-stunned face when, seeming willing to answer even her smallest query, 'To go back to the beginning,' he replied, 'it makes for efficiency in my working life for me to employ only the best qualified people. So, with that instinctive in me, I began interviewing a succession of very highly certificated women for the temporary job I'd advertised.'

'It—um—must have been a bit of a shock when I turned up—not a qualification in sight and, according to my mother, looking like a gypsy,' Fabienne commented quietly, then swallowed again at his warm look and quickly asked, 'Why did you pick me?'

'I asked myself the same question many times that day. You obviously didn't care whether you got the job or not and, just as obviously since you turned down reimbursement of expenses, you weren't financially in need. Against that, though, you said you came from a very happy family—to my mind that augured well to help Rachel and her children be a happy family again. Perhaps you might be able to make Rachel feel a shade more secure, a shade less depressed. You'd said you were good friends with your eight-year-old nephew—so maybe someone who could offer friendliness to Kitty and John might be a better qualification than the paper ones you lacked.'

'Oh,' she breathed softly and, her heart palpitating like crazy as she looked at him, she had her head nowhere near together and could only think to say, 'S-so, once I'd passed investigation, you rang me and offered me the job.'

'And, ridiculously I thought, found that my heart was beating that bit faster just to hear your voice.'

'Honestly!' she exclaimed on a squeak of sound. 'But—but you were so—um—short with me over the phone when you rang.'

'How else would I be?' Vere questioned. 'I barely knew you, and it *was* ridiculous. In fact,' he went on, 'there have been countless times since I've known you when I've thought my feelings, my actions, to be absurd in the extreme.' Fabienne was hanging on his every word, and she stared at him with huge brown eyes. 'Oh, dear life,' he breathed as he looked deeply into her eyes, 'I'm absolutely desperate to kiss you—yet at the same time I'm terrified I've got it all wrong.'

Oh, grief, Fabienne panicked. She wanted him to kiss her, wanted to be held close to him, to be secure in his arms. But secure was just *not* what she was feeling just then. Even though Vere had told her that she held his whole heart it seemed so impossible that she needed to know more, quite a lot more, before she dared to let go the brake she was holding on her normally spontaneous emotions.

'I'd—um——' She tried hard not to swallow again, but found that she just had to before she could carry on. 'I'd l-like to hear about your absurd actions,' she requested.

'Dear Fenne,' he breathed, and it was every bit as if he understood the quagmire of hopes and fears, doubts and dreams she was going through. For, as if he just could not resist it, he placed a gentle kiss on her forehead and, as she clutched once more at his hands, 'Was it not absurd,' he asked, 'that, when I had only seen you for about fifteen minutes on the previous Wednesday, I should know myself oddly unsettled as I waited for you to arrive the following Sunday?'

'But—you weren't here when I arrived that first Sunday.'

'Did I not say absurd? Damn the woman, I thought—and went out.'

'I wasn't sure what time I was expected to arrive,' Fabienne explained in a hurry. 'And then it took longer for me to find Sutton Ash than I thought.'

'But you did arrive, thank God. And in no time—the very next day in fact—I was on the receiving end of some of your spirit. When you challenged me—did I want you to leave?—I realised that I found your sparking eyes, the whole mien of you, more stimulating than anything I'd known just lately.'

'Truly?' she whispered, her gaze fixed to his.

'Most definitely truly,' he replied softly. 'From there I began to discover a whole crop of emotions new to me. Was it jealousy—of course not—that I didn't care for some man in the village asking you out?'

'You were jealous—of Lyndon Davies?' she asked in astonishment.

'Not only him, any man who rang you here.'

'Tom Walton?'

'That'd be the one,' he confirmed, and went on before she could blink, 'Did you have to go out with Lyndon Davies on Monday?'

Good heavens, he really *had* been jealous! Fabienne's confidence that Vere really had been speaking the truth when he'd said she held his whole heart grew by leaps and bounds.

'I didn't *have* to go out with him, no,' she replied, and took a deep breath and grabbed at a handful of courage to tell him, 'But it hurt so much when I saw you with your arm around Rachel's shoulders that I knew I just couldn't sit down at the same dinner table with the two of you.'

'My dear!' Vere exclaimed, but Fabienne had to hurry on while she still had the courage.

'So I rang Lyndon Davies—whose invitation to a jazz concert I'd turned down earlier—and accepted, if he'd let me take him to dinner first.'

'Sweetheart!' Vere cried in wonder. 'You love me!'

She had known that, with his quick-thinking brain, from her 'it hurt so much' he would soon have worked that out. But—and she owned everything was happening so fast—she was more than a mite confused. Did he, with his, 'you who hold my whole heart', mean that he loved her?

'I f-feel the same way about you that you feel about me,' she told him nervously—and was gently but firmly drawn towards him.

'Then we, my love,' he breathed, his face close to hers, 'are in love with each other.'

'Vere!' she gasped.

'Fabienne, my love!' he murmured, and he lowered his head, and kissed her. And, one kiss never enough, it was quite some while before, while still holding her in his arms, he drew back to look at her. Gently he traced the curve of her love-warmed face with a finger. 'My darling, we've so much to talk over—and here I am, yet again in danger of losing my head.'

'Oh, why not?' she gasped.

Vere laughed. 'My stars, did I say I was going to have trouble with you?' He did not wait for her reply but said, his laughter fading, 'First of all, let's establish that I love you with everything that's in me.'

'Oh, Vere,' Fabienne cried, and even though she had more confidence it still seemed impossible.

'And you—you love me?'

'Yes,' she replied—and discovered she was again strangely shy.

'You wouldn't like to say so, I suppose.'

'Oh, I do love you,' she managed bravely, and was oh, so tenderly kissed, a beautiful reward for her courage.

'How long?' Vere wanted to know.

Shyness, most peculiar when she had always considered herself thoroughly outgoing, was there to trip her up again. 'You first,' she pleaded.

And Vere smiled down, more wonderfully understanding than she had realised and, tucking her securely in his right arm, he began. 'It had been growing, I now see, from that first meeting. Nothing one could take hold of, just having you on my mind, feeling unsettled waiting for you to turn up to start work. Observing your fine sensitivity, the way that, without pressurising Rachel you seemed to be easing her out of herself.'

'I think my brother may have had a lot to do with that,' interrupted Fabienne, pointing it out on realising that it must be so.

'Don't underestimate your powers, sweet love. Though it was your power over me that, within the week, was causing me to doubt my judgement.'

Fabienne owned she was totally fascinated by what he had just said. 'How?'

'Do you remember the end of your first week here?'

'I've forgotten nothing,' she replied softly.

Vere dropped a light kiss to the corner of her mouth, and seemed to lose himself for a moment or two and looked lovingly into her face. Then he recollected, 'Then you'll remember we'd fired up at each other when you asked when your weekend started—and I again felt a nip of jealousy that you were rushing off to some man-friend.'

'Good grief!' she gasped. 'I can't believe it!'

'No more could I. Nor could I believe I could be so vile as to have dinner out, knowing perfectly well from what I'd seen of you that there was no way you would leave the children and go home to Lintham that Friday night with me not there.'

'You wretch!' she berated him—but was smiling.

'I agree,' he smiled back. 'But for my sins I felt more disturbed than young John that night.'

'He had a nightmare.'

'And you must have been into his room in a flash. You got there before me anyhow,' he recalled, 'and I looked at you and knew you were beautiful both inside and out.'

'Oh, Vere,' Fabienne sighed—no one had ever said such a lovely thing to her before.

'Is it any wonder,' he continued, 'that, after we'd left John, I should stand with you outside your room and feel such a desperate urge to take you in my arms that I just had to question whether you *had* been the right choice to bring into my home? Not from the point of view of the children—but mine, and my peace of mind.'

'And I never knew!' she gasped. 'Um——'

'Go on,' Vere urged. 'If you've a confession I'd love to hear it.'

'You're too smart,' she returned, but confessed, 'Um—if it's of any interest—without you so much as touching me that night I was never more aware of any man as I was you. I—er—think I wanted you to kiss me.'

A superb grin lit his mouth, his eyes. 'Allow me to remedy that omission,' he breathed, and tenderly pulled her closer to him, his head coming down. Their lips met, and Fabienne went slightly out of control for long seconds as Vere moulded her to him—and passion soared as they kissed and kissed again.

A shaken breath of sound left her when at last he broke his kiss and pulled back. 'Oh, Vere,' she gasped, her voice a mere thread of sound. 'I n-never knew I could, that you...that I...'

'It's pretty shattering, isn't it?' he agreed, giving her the tenderest of looks. 'But I'm being unfair, my darling.' Somehow they were half lying with each other on the couch. Manfully he moved them until they were both sitting more or less the same way they had been before they had lost their heads a little. 'Remind me where I was,' he growled.

'You expect me to remember, after *that*?'

'It's what you do to me, woman,' he declared throatily to her delight.

She positively beamed at him for his trouble, but made tremendous efforts to recall, 'You said you wanted to take me in your arms that night John had a nightmare—so why were you like a bear with a sore head only a few hours later at breakfast?'

'You looked stunning—and were lippy with it—and I had just realised that I'd hardly seen you all week but, dammit, now that I was free for the weekend, you were off. I'd just realised I didn't want you to go away—how else should I act?' She could not help it—she just had to kiss him. 'Dear God,' he groaned, 'if ever there was a threat to a man's sanity, it's you.'

'You say the nicest things,' she murmured.

'Witch!' he tossed at her and kissed her nose. 'So I waited all that infernal, damp weekend,' he went on, 'and you, thank God, came back, and I'm at once alive again. There you are, all flashing eyes and temper——'

'Who provoked it?' she wanted to know.

'Who but me?' he agreed. 'Though I did get up on Monday feeling that there wasn't too much wrong with my world—and for a bonus went to work with the sound of your laughter in my ears. Laughter, I only then realised, had been a stranger at Brackendale recently. So,' Vere ended, looking adoringly at her, 'gradually, and without being aware of what was happening, I began to fall more and more in love with this woman who turned my world upside-down.'

'Me?' Fabienne questioned cheerfully.

'Who else but you?' he laughed. 'Who else but you makes me want to kiss you one minute, and sort you out the next? Who else but you, after I *have* kissed you, makes me decide I'd better dine away from home—just in case I can't resist the urge to do it again?'

'No!' she gasped. 'You dined out because of me?'

'Frequently,' he admitted. 'And last Thursday, solely because of you, I didn't come home at all.'

'Because of me?'

'You, my dear, were really getting to me by then. But little good it did me not coming home Thursday, because by Friday I began to be afraid that you might have decided to leave for Lintham before I could get back. I rush back, hear from Mrs Hobbs that you're still here—and, incidentally, of your endless patience with the twins that day and the day before—then there you are, having come to find me in this very room. Yet, while I'm still delighting in having you so close, in how lovely you are, you dare to tell me that you'll be taking Kitty, John and Rachel to Lintham the next day—and nobody's asking me if I'd like to come, too.'

'You wanted to come with us!'

'I didn't see why I should be deprived of your company! Which, since to avoid seeing you I'd deliberately not come home the night before,' he added with a slightly self-deprecating look, 'was when I started to realise that something was happening to my powers of logic.' He smiled. 'I was not at all ready to admit the strength of the hold you had on me, yet couldn't help knowing how good you were with Kitty and John, and how only since you came Rachel seemed to be surfacing from her depression. And how—selfishly, I own—life was much smoother for me now that you were here.'

'I didn't know I was *that* good.'

'Minx. In my view, you were just about perfect for the job. Yet, if I allowed this spell you were weaving over me full rein, it could all end with you leaving.'

'How?' She asked her favourite question.

'How else? Just supposing,' he put to her, 'that—at its furthest extent—we had an affair. How would it end?

Amicably? What if not? I'd noticed about you a fine sensitivity, and also a fire of splendid spirit. I neither wanted to hurt you—nor end up enemies.' Vere's look was steady on hers when he said, his voice throaty once more, 'Only recently, my very dear Fabienne, have I realised that it isn't an affair I want with you.'

'It—isn't?' she choked, her eyes glued to the sincerity in his.

Slowly, he shook his head. 'What I want, above everything, I've realised, is to—marry you.'

'Marry me!' she whispered.

'You wouldn't be so cruel as to tell me "no"?'

'I...' Her throat went dry and she could not continue.

'Please, Fenne,' he said grittily. 'Last night I knew I was not a man to—as you put it—beg for sexual favours. But if I have to beg you to marry me, that I will, willingly...'

'Oh, darling!' She hurriedly found her voice. 'You have to beg nothing from me.'

'You'll marry me?'

'Oh, yes, I'd love to.'

'Darling!'

There was silence in the room for a long time as gently he kissed her, and tenderly he whispered her name and showered her with endearments.

'Oh, sweet love.' He pulled back so that he could see into her face. 'I tried, one Sunday when you were later returning than I thought you should be, to lock you out of my house—and found, as I waited for you to come home, that I just couldn't lock you out of my head. I followed that up by intimating that I'd put an end to your walking—as you put it—the hallowed halls of Brackendale by sacking you, and for my sins grew terrified that you'd thumb your nose at me and wouldn't be there when I returned that night.'

'But you knew I would be—that was the day you rang to speak to Rachel.'

'That was the day I invented a need to speak to Rachel and rang, fearful that you'd already left. I just had to know that you were still there before I could find any sort of concentration to deal with anything. Even so, I had to leave the office early to come home to check that you were still here.'

'You love me that much!'

'Oh, so much more, but it was only on Monday—Monday morning to be exact—that I faced up to what has seen me jealous of every man you've been in contact with. Even Alex, until I learned from the twins that the man you were kissing was your brother.'

'That makes me feel a bit better for being jealous over Rachel.'

'Has it been hell for you too, love?'

'Murder,' she owned happily. But just had to ask, 'When, when did you know, Vere?'

'On Monday, my love,' he told her without hesitation. 'I'd had a foul weekend without you, and tried to take it out on you when everybody seemed as happy as the devil when you arrived from Lintham. Crass, wasn't it?' He grinned. 'I'd ached for you all over the weekend, yet the moment I see you and what do I do but go for your jugular—talking all that rot about the children having to be up for school in the morning...'

'And hearing me boast that they would be, and——'

'And all the time we're arguing I'm fighting the alarming pull that's getting the better of me, to kiss you into submission.'

'Really!' she gasped. 'You ordered me out of your sight—fast,' she remembered.

'What else should I do? There I am fighting hard against the need to kiss you, when you deeply offend my manhood by thinking I might hit you—and yet still I wanted to kiss your rebellious mouth.'

'I'm sorry I offended you,' she apologised at once. 'If it's any consolation, I worked out during that long and sleepless night that you were probably as appalled as I was by the suggestion.'

Her apology was accepted unequivocally. 'You were sleepless, too?' he smiled.

'I was awake for hours and hours,' she admitted, and added with a grin, 'Which is why I was sound away when you came into my room when you returned home for your briefcase.'

'Er—that was a lie,' he confessed.

'A lie?'

Vere nodded, but was not looking at all shamefaced as he further confessed, 'I returned home after dropping the twins off at school for no other reason than I had a compulsion—a compulsion so strong I could not ignore it—to see you.'

'Oh, Vere!' she cried on a sigh of a breath.

'"Oh, Vere" it was, when—and I did knock at your door, albeit only lightly before I came in—I saw you lying there in sleep, your hair all mussed up, your face angelic. I don't know for how long I just stood looking at your beautiful face before I called your name. When you were awake and I came and sat on your bed—then I knew.'

'That you loved me?'

'Much more than that, my precious love. I discovered that I'm deeply in love with you, that I absolutely adore you, and I also discover—this never having happened to me before—that I just don't know how to deal with it. So——' he smiled '—I tore myself away, thought about you all day, about how I hadn't known you for so very long yet how marvellous was every new thing I learned about you, and of how, whether I'd known you two minutes or two years, you were so right for me.'

'You came home early.'

'Since I've known you, it's started to become a habit.'

'You came home early to see me?' she queried, her heart racing in her delight.

'But of course. And,' he went on, 'had a splendid excuse to have a couple of days off work and to spend yet more time with you when Rachel said she would like to leave the children while she went and made peace with her parents.'

'Oh, how dreadful of me!' Fabienne exclaimed. 'I told you that wouldn't be necessary!'

'Not only that, heartless woman,' he complained, 'but, to add insult to injury, you caused me rage and jealousy such as I've never known by daring to take yourself off that night with another man!'

'Are you going to forgive me?'

'I forgave you the very next day when you and the twins came singing round the corner and, with my heart hammering like thunder, I thought I saw something in your unguarded look that said you might feel something for me that might—dare I hope?—be a little warmer than liking.'

'I did wonder if I'd been caught out,' she murmured, and Vere placed a tender kiss on the side of her mouth.

'Afterwards I couldn't be certain of what I'd seen,' he admitted. 'But, at dinner last night, I was aware of you every minute I was talking to either Kitty or John, and wondering how to get to know you better. I decided to ask you to join me in this room later.'

'You wanted to see me to get to know me better!' she exclaimed.

'That was one of the very good reasons,' he confirmed. 'The other was that having you in the same house was not enough. I wanted you in the same room with me. Though I wasn't above using the children as an excuse—even when I could see for myself how they were thriving,' he owned, going on to admit further, 'I, my darling, started to grow terrified of frightening you off if I said too much too soon.'

'You didn't.'

'Believe it,' Vere assured her. 'But so much for my thinking we'd get to know each other better. In no time jealousy is rearing its ugly head over your jazz concert friend. When you said something about there being a lot of things you liked of which I knew nothing I tried to get back to where we were. I was about to suggest that perhaps it might be an idea if I did get to know more of what you liked—that maybe we should get to know one another—when you're on your feet and off to bed!'

'Not before I'd been served with a helping of jealousy myself.'

'How?' It was his turn to enquire.

'You told me Rachel had phoned, and——'

'My love—she only rang to ask if the twins were all right.'

'Which, of course,' Fabienne smiled, able then to own, 'is no more than any parent would do in the same circumstances.'

Vere looked tenderly at her, seemed unable then to resist kissing her, but was holding her safe in the harbour of his arms when he asked, 'Do I get to know when you knew you were in love with me?'

'Certainly,' Fabienne replied. 'Though from the very first there was something there—I found you a very disturbing man, Mr Tolladine.'

'I like it,' he grinned. She grinned, too. She could not help it—life was wonderful, Vere was wonderful. 'When?' he demanded.

'Sunday,' she replied at once.

'Last Sunday?'

Fabienne nodded. 'I'd driven from my parents aware of an anxiety to get back here—plagued by thoughts of whether Rachel and Alex had fallen for each other and how I didn't want you to be hurt—when suddenly there you were, and I knew then that it wasn't Brackendale I'd wanted to get back to, but you. That I was in love with you, and had been for quite some time.'

'Little love,' Vere crooned, and rained kisses over her face.

'That wasn't what you called me that night,' she smiled.

'Are you going to forgive me?'

'Done,' she obliged, and was kissed again before Vere pulled back and looked lovingly down into her face.

'That was another night when I didn't get much sleep,' he owned. 'Though, since knowing you, my sleep pattern seems to have gone totally haywire.'

'Was it because of me that you couldn't sleep last night? You—um—said that you couldn't.'

'Both before and after,' he replied meaningfully.

'Ah,' she murmured.

'Indeed,' he smiled. 'Before, thoughts of you were haunting me, keeping me sleepless. Afterwards, when I'd left you, the hold I'd got on my sanity seemed very precarious. It just didn't seem possible from what I knew of you that you could respond the way you had and not feel *something* for me. True, you'd let me know in no uncertain terms that you'd prefer to have your bed to yourself. But whatever it was that had triggered your last-minute refusal—and jealousy over Rachel, I confess, was not one of the answers I came up with——' he paused and bestowed a light kiss to her mouth '—you had to care something for me, didn't you? I then recalled that look in your eyes when you'd come across me unexpectedly yesterday and——'

'And you decided to find out.'

'It was either that or go completely off my head.'

'Oh, darling,' she cried. 'And I was late coming back from taking Kitty and John to school.'

'And when you do get back, you very nearly give me heart failure by saying that you want to leave.'

'I'm sorry,' she apologised prettily.

'I'll forgive you on one condition.'

'Anything,' she promised blindly.

'Good. Then we'll be married without delay.'

'Oh, Vere.'

He kissed her and then whispered, 'My wonderful darling. I have a vivid memory of one day when I was again home early watching you and the twins in the teeming rain coming boisterously up the drive. When I realised you weren't coming in the front way, I found myself somehow moved from the drawing-room to be at the rear to meet you.'

'Oh!' she gasped in surprise, and smiled as she softly added, 'I remember that day.'

'There you were, damp, beautiful, mischievous and, I thought, absolutely delightful.'

'You kissed me.'

'And you returned the compliment,' he replied with a rueful grin. 'Promise me something else.'

'Again—anything.'

'I want our children to be just like you—promise you'll teach them to eat ice-creams in the rain.'

She laughed joyously—she loved him.

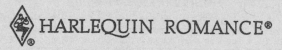

HARLEQUIN ROMANCE®

brings you

More Romances Celebrating Love, Families and Children!

Harlequin Romance #3362

THE BABY BUSINESS

by

Rebecca Winters

If you love babies—this book is for you!

When hotel nanny Rachel Ellis searches for her lost brother, she meets his boss—the dashing and gorgeous Vincente de Raino. She is unprepared for her strong attraction to him, but even more unprepared to be left holding the baby—his adorable baby niece, Luisa, who makes her long for a baby of her own!

Available in May wherever Harlequin Books are sold.

MILLION DOLLAR SWEEPSTAKES (III)

HARLEQUIN ROMANCE®

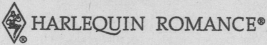

brings you

Harlequin Romance #3361, *Mail-Order Bridegroom*,
in our Sealed with a Kiss series next month is by one of
our most popular authors, Day Leclaire.

Leah Hampton needs a husband for her ranch
to survive—a strictly no-nonsense business arrangement.
Advertising for one in the local newspaper makes good
sense, but she finds to her horror a reply from none other
than Hunter Pryde, the man she had been in love with
eight years before!

Is her fate sealed with one kiss? Or can she resist falling
in love with him all over again?

In the coming months, look for these exciting
Sealed with a Kiss stories:

Harlequin Romance #3366
P.S. I Love You by Valerie Parv in June

Harlequin Romance #3369
Wanted: Wife and Mother by Barbara McMahon in July

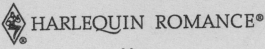 HARLEQUIN ROMANCE®

celebrates

FAMILY TIES!

**Join us in June for our brand-new miniseries—
Family Ties!**

Family... What does it bring to mind? The trials and
pleasures of children and grandchildren, loving parents
and close bonds with brothers and sisters—that special
joy a close family can bring. Whatever meaning it has for
you, we know you'll enjoy these heartwarming love stories
in which we celebrate family—and in which you can
meet some fascinating members of our
heroes' and heroines' families.

The first title to look out for is...
Simply the Best
by Catherine Spencer

followed by...

Make Believe Marriage
by Renee Roszel in July

FT-G-R